And the Rest is History

But the Best is Her Story

ONCE UPON A TIME

I0847377

B J A-ELLIOTT

Entegrity Choice Publishing
PO Box 453
Powder Springs, GA 30127
info@entegritypublishing.com
www.entegritypublishing.com
770.727.6517

Printed in the United States of America

Library of Congress Cataloging-in-Publication Data
ISBN: 979-8-9850792-9-6
Library of Congress Control Number: 2025907426

Dedication

This book, with all of its stories is dedicated to the next generation of young women, their daughters, their granddaughters and beyond. We want you to realize that the things we will share, are real, from things passed down to us, and from our own life experiences. Our principles are not just *weird* **"old school directives,"** but *"absolutes"* as we believe. We want you to know that we see you and God's plan for your future, so you won't have to wait for the middle/late stage of your life (36–65 years), to take a deep cleansing breath, hold, exhale and then breathe again. I've heard it said, **"Don't just count your days, but make your days count."**

It has been noted that there are stages of life span. "Life stages are the phases from birth to death through which we develop and grow. Each stage covers an age range during which most people share common interests, desires, feelings, thoughts, experiences, values, and of course, a level of maturity."

Contents

Dedication   iii

Foreword   vii

Acknowledgments   ix

Preface   xi

1   *Annie and Frank's Love Story*   1

2   *Lernice and Louie's Love Story*   5

3   *Linda and James's Love Story*   9

4   *Bev and Lee's Love Story*   13

5   *Dorothy and Caselle's Love Story*   38

6   *Jacque and (Robert) Bob's Love Story*   42

7   *Ja'nye and Pete's Love Story*   47

8   *Jeanette and Keith's Love Story*   86

9   *Barbara and James's Love Story*   93

10   *Ann and Albert's Love Story*   100

11   *Deloise and Alfred's Love Story*   103

12   *Joanne and Victor's Love Story*   108

13   *Janiese and Cody's Love Story*   114

14   *Judith and Wilson's Love Story*   116

15   *Lisa and Michael's Love Story*   119

16   *Stephanie and Anthony's Love Story*   122

Accolades from her professors from Beulah Heights University
which speaks to her writing, the skill for which she gives homage
to her 11th grade teacher, Ms. Burke, from Copiague HS,
in NY.

Beulah Heights University Praises for writing skills.
This week, your post continued to go beyond excellence!
What can I say! EXCELLENCE at its best! What a great
tool for the class to glean from this post! Your defining,
knowledge and insight on this week's post is dynamic!
—Prof. Dr. Bowen

Based on your gifted abilities to articulate your thoughts,
keep reading, always posture yourself to learn, and you will
always have something to write.
—Master's Graduate W. Harmon

You are a writer! I am not surprised to learn that you are
writing newsletters regularly for church etc. Keep at it.
I will be buying your books one day!
—Prof. Dr. Abram

17	*Marion and Albert's (June) Love Story*	131
18	*Ambrozine and Cyril's Love Story*	134
19	*Aunt Sylvia and Uncle Alan's Love Story*	140
20	*Brenda and Tony's Love Story*	147
21	*Debra and Alfred's Love Story*	151
22	*Diane and Clemet's Love Story*	154
23	*Gabrielle and Lex's—My First Love Story*	156
24	*Addie and Norman's Love Story*	159
25	*Marliss and Jay's Love Story*	163

HONORABLE MENTION:
Celebrating Full Gospel Pastors — 172

HONORABLE MENTION:
Celebrating My Favorite Cousin — 174

HONORABLE MENTION:
Celebrating My Best Friends and Superheroes — 176

HONORABLE MENTION:
Celebrating My Former Pastors—Amityville Full Gospel Tabernacle — 178

HONORABLE MENTION:
Celebrating My Friends and Superheroes — 180

"What I've learned is that when you find a thing that produces a feeling of peace or joy, try to hold onto it. It's like bliss. That's music for me."
—*Paul Simon*

When asked by someone, "What do you want to be when you grow up?" Her sweet answer was: "In Love."
—*Jennifer Lopez*

Foreword

As I sit in my room today, at 80 years of age, under the watchful eye of my caretakers, it is hard to believe the span of time that has whizzed by, almost five decades as memory serves me. Our meeting allowed Bev and I to become community co-laborers, then friends on a level that has destined each of us with purpose.

Under the employ of NYU, I along with two trainers from California and Washington, DC, were called upon to train a group of Head Start family counselors to facilitate the government program "Exploring Parenting." Away at a private retreat in the mountains, Bev was part of that one-week intense training session. I found her to be warm and delightful. Having charismatic abilities, she went on to facilitate many groups across the Long Island community for many years. I witnessed her groups, relationships, and as they blossomed, so did she. Her dedication ran deep, and her connection to the people, both men and women, were genuinely and sincerely heartfelt.

It is because of this endeavor that I am intensely proud to introduce this seasoned citizen, writing her first book, a compilation of love stories to the world. As her mentor, I have discovered her humility, sincerity, and sensitivity toward the human race to be nothing less than uplifting. She has graciously had her hand on the pulse of women since the days of her facilitating "Exploring Parenting" groups in New York and Georgia. Her connections remained strong. After a brief separation, Bev found me again and continued to reach out and remain connected, though we were miles apart. She often tells me how much she has still been inspired by our conversations and wants everyone around me to know the power and influence that I have put into the universe. She doesn't allow me to forget the blood, sweat, tears, and the work I've done, the lives I've touched, and this makes our friendship so precious to me. Her work continues to show and share historically, the lives of women from this century, and from the past, that we give to those beyond. Today I feel such an emotional bond that fuels my present writing.

These remarkable stories of past love, let us peek into what love meant to women from all walks of life and established the feel, like you were presently sitting in the room. After you have laughed and maybe cried a little, it will inspire you to hold love close and to respect the origin of it.

So, journey with her, insomuch as you will desire more. The conclusions will be found in her second book entitled *Loss and Found*. You too will find she is unafraid to speak truth with passion and stand up for what she believes to be right.

Ms. Marilyn Bartlett—NYU Professor Emeritus
Mentor/Friend
Profound speaker and successful leadership trainer
Certified Consultant advocating strong families through the
    Head Start Program

Acknowledgments

I want to thank my **Heavenly Father**, for keeping me safe and alive, to fulfill His purpose through me. Then for keeping my mind right. I thank Him for allowing me to have many encounters, with ability and strength to *swim upstream*, *against* what folk say is the norm and of a popular opinion. **Rev. John D. Lawrence** once stated that "any old dead fish could go *downstream*."

I'm grateful for my **earthly Father** who pushed me to stand strong in what I believed, and realizing my own strength and importance when I walked in a room, only because the Spirit of God was walking with me. Then knowing without Him, I could do nothing. I recognize, His Spirit was on *fleek*, and that's what you can take to the bank, with a check you can cash now. *"That part."*

I want to take the time to thank the two gentlemen that took part in writing their story on behalf of their wives, who were unable to write at this time. So, guess who. Then giving a shout out to Minister L. Hankins, for her contribution and support in this endeavor.

Preface

Awwhh . . . I found a love. Well, that's what most people dream of, "finding love." Young little girls have been obsessed for centuries with the story that begins **"Once upon a Time"** in the storyline, and of meeting their **knight** in shining armor, then riding off into the **sunset**, living **happily ever after**. Is this actually how the universe framed our lives? Some folks say you're born that way, to **believe in fairy tales**. Sometimes, it's that "ever after" that changes or is interrupted. However, "happily ever after" doesn't come so easily.

In these stories many hoped to find their one true love, and most did.

Some marriages did not end parting by death but in separation and divorce, but at least **for a moment, it was love.**

In this new era of time however, society has **redefined** how people find and fall in love. The dating process is off the charts as to who you will date, how you find a mate, as it relates to race, **gender** and dating sites. They have even included something called the **Later-Dater**. The dating pool is at best complicated and confusing. Some, "Catfish," others put their best foot forward, while others don't keep it 100 and don't tell the truth in conversation. They are not up front about what they expect in a relationship. Too much texting and in boxing.

No "real" conversation, only saying what sounds good at the time, tickling the ear. Many times, religious belief is the last thing they inquire about.

One generation of men searched for a Proverbs 31 woman, and that generation of women were in search of their Boaz, both lacking "substance." We have a generation now that says, "what's Love Got to do with it." They behave like it, and they build upon . . . , well I don't really know what. Now what can I say about A I which is now on the scene, seemingly the future of love and communication today. I pray that the pendulum will swing back in the direction of normal.

Let's see where these loves will take us, maybe even down the yellow brick road, and some, maybe just the plain "old school way."

We are in the state of flux, wherein we will have to make certain choices, which will affect the rest of our lives and that of our next generations. Remember how we live our life will affect our legacy. Right now, I feel that we are failing in passing down what we believe and what we know to be right. Pastor Marvin Winans said in a song, "Somebody's Got to Tell Them."

From the beginning of time, God had **a path, a plan, and a purpose,** all we needed to do was to walk in it. He ordained man and woman to come together. If we tell the truth, we all aren't really doing that part, or maybe I should just say, we just need to do better, especially after watching the news and seeing what 15-year-old girls are doing these days (ref. Madison, Wisconsin). Somebody **better** tell them.

Many promise to stand by you, until there was no more breath left in them . . . an endless love, however it doesn't always work out that way, especially if you don't actually put the work in. Forever love doesn't happen by magic. If you want a long and lasting love, it will take work, **hard work**, on both sides. Somebody has to tell them that part. It is certainly not all sunshine and roses. It is a constant decision to "Love." Love and forgiveness are decisions, not a feeling but a daily action. You will need both in any relationship. If you hold on to the wrongs, it will hurt you physically, emotionally and spiritually.

Here's how their stories begin . . .
How they fell in love.

1

Annie and Frank's Love Story

It was the summer of 1989. I was leaving my job at the local mall. As I was waiting at the bus stop with my friend and while we were talking, over my shoulder I heard someone say hello, my name is Frank. He had walked up behind me. He stuttered, "My naammme is Frank, whatttts your naamme?" I thought in my mind if you don't get away from me you better! I said my name and I quickly turned my back to face my friend. As I turned the bus arrived and I stepped in front of my friend to hurriedly get on the bus. I made sure my friend sat next to me, and I continued talk to her until the bus came to my stop.

After our initial encounter and after spotting him a few more times at that bus stop, I tried everything I could to stay as far away from him as I could. I changed my bus route, and I even moved at one point! I did not want anything to do with him. First of all, he had what I called, pork chop sideburns. They came down the side of his face, beginning small and grew larger as they went down to his chin and met his beard. Also, I thought he was too old.

One day while I was riding on my new bus route, it made a stop. Low and behold who got on the bus? Yes, you got it! It was him again! My heart just sank! I knew he was going to come and sit next to me because I always sat next to the window. I quickly pulled out my Bible and pretended to read it so that way I wouldn't have to talk to him. As soon as I got to my stop, I jumped up so fast I almost knocked him off the seat trying to get away. I thought to myself next time I will catch the bus at a different time. It was some time shortly after that, I moved to an apartment with a coworker. Some months went by, and I thought surely, I'm free at last!

One evening after work I got on the bus going to my new apartment, and my friend Rita was on the bus. We started chatting and she said I know someone who really wants to get to know you and they really think you are cute. She had my full attention! She told me that he was a good man, a hard worker and he was good looking too. Now I really sat up straight and could not wait for more. She said they worked at the same place. When she told me his name I was completely deflated! I thought Lord, what have I done to deserve this? Rita kept talking and pleading with me to give him a chance. Finally, I said "okay and if this does not work out, don't blame me."

I gave her my number to give to him, unknowingly that I had one number wrong. It was not intentional because it was a new number. I heard from her the next day. She said that he had called me and said that you must be playing tricks, because he called the number several times and a man answered. The man violently threatened him if he didn't stop calling. Rita asked me, "What number did you give him?" I told her that if it was the wrong number, it was not on purpose. It was a new number. Then I gave her the correct number and sure enough he called me the very next night. We talked for a while, and I expressed my issues with him, and he corrected them right away.

I finally settled myself into getting to know him, and he was a good man after all. We started dating, and it was now October 1989. After dating for two months, he asked me what I wanted for Christmas. Me being a practical girl, I said I needed an alarm clock. That is exactly what I got. It was my first gift! He purchased a nice one by GE, a clock radio and I still have it to this day, and it still works.

We dated only nine months before we were married. We got married on September 16, 1990 and our marriage lasted just shy of 30 years. That's only because he got sick and passed away. He was a good man, and he didn't drink or use drugs. For that matter, neither did I. However, he was a prankster, and he enjoyed pulling his devious pranks on me.

One day I was not feeling well, and I was at home alone in the bedroom lying down. I didn't hear Frank come into the house, but I heard someone trying to open the bedroom door. I was so glad I had it locked. The knob kept rattling and shaking! I was scared, so I slid off the bed to the floor and called 911. I told them someone had broken into my house. They were about to send the police but then he called out and said it was him. It was just in the nick of time that I got to tell the operator it was husband and don't send anyone. But now, I was certainly going to get him back. When I let him in the room, I said to him, "you just better stay on high alert because your day is coming."

I kept my word. One afternoon he was in the shower, and he left the bathroom door open. I tiptoed just up to the shower curtain and snatched it open; I yelled GOTCHA! It was so loud that He fell flat against the shower wall, eyes bucked wide open. I laughed so hard I fell to the floor. We played pranks on each other so many times and we would always laugh and talk about it later. The only thing that we had that was opposite was, I was a people person and liked to be on the go. He was a homebody.

When we had been married for about seven years, I said to my husband, "we need to talk." I didn't like going out without him, even though he gave me permission to do so. Thankfully, we came to a compromise. I would stay home with him one weekend and the next weekend we would have to go out. It was difficult at first because he would go out with me, but only to go eat and come back home. We would go to places that were not so crowded. I accepted that. The more we went out the better it got. I would stay home with him and just watch TV or do whatever he wanted to do. Checkers was his game, and he would beat me every time. Being together, was all that really mattered to me, and we enjoyed being with each other. I realized that marriage takes work, if you really want it to work. It's all about listening with your heart and not just your ears. I learned to conversate with kindness and understanding.

2

Lernice and Louie's Love Story

Let's rewind to the early 2000's when life was a whirlwind of pediatric residency chaos. In the midst of my hectic schedule, enter Stacie, my childhood friend with a flair for divine match-making. Now, Stacy's divine interventions, or so she believed, led me to a guy named Louie. At the time, love wasn't exactly on my radar. I was already dealing with a long-distance college boyfriend, and my main focus was navigating the challenges of residency. Yet, here comes Stacie, insisting I meet Louie, who was a friend of her husbands from way back. The universe has its ways, right? Now, picture this: a dinner at her parents' house. This was the setting for our first encounter. I'm there, not particularly interested, not engaging in deep conversations. Post dinner, Stacie drops the bomb shell. Louie is seriously interested in me and just for kicks, Stacie's husband is doing the bro-code matchmaking on the other end, telling Louie the same.

Flashback to my late twenties—Louie is in his early thirties, and I'm trying to stick to my rule of not dating guys with kids.

Yet, Louie is making it increasingly difficult for me to adhere to that principle. Now we found ourselves going on double dates, picnics, and Broadway shows. Then Louie introduces me to the wonders of the Seven Lakes in Rockland County.

We began sharing endless conversations, even delving into his past. Then the real matchmaking begins when Stacie convinced me to share my contact information with Louie. Subsequently, hours of phone calls follow, covering everything from his previous marriage and divorced life to the heartwarming desire to reunite with his children. As our connection deepens, so does our time together. These times included movies, dinners, and thoughtful gestures that made it hard to resist the genuine care he showed.

Then comes the unexpected an outing to the Seven Lakes, where Louie experiences difficulty breathing. Concerned, I push for medical care, and we end up in a Bronx urgent care, which turned into a long night. His gratitude for my support marks a turning point for us, and from there on, every point and every day off, becomes an opportunity for an adventure or quiet moments, building a connection beyond the surface.

And so, Louie becomes a constant in my life, proving that sometimes, love finds its way into our hearts when we least expect it. I found myself succumbing to Louie's charm. Despite my initial rule about not dating someone with children, his sincerity, generosity, and unwavering commitment started to erode my reservations. It turned out he was not just a gentleman, but also a mentor to his godbrother, imparting to him valuable life lessons.

As the months passed, Louie introduced me to his family, and it was time for him to meet mine. Louie's genuine warmth and magnetic personality won over everyone he encountered. Within just a month of dating, he gifted me an Italian gold necklace as a symbol of his commitment—an emblem I still cherish to this day.

Despite our differences—cultural and linguistic—Louie's mother welcomed me into their family with open arms. Her unintentional announcement to her neighbors about her "adopted daughter-in-law," became a humorous anecdote, highlighting the cultural disparities we navigated with grace and laughter.

Louie continued to surprise and delight me with his spontaneity, from introducing me to the UniverSoul Circus and with each passing day, my initial reservations faded, replaced by a genuine appreciation for the man who had become an integral part of my life. Throughout our relationship, Louie proved that love doesn't always adhere to rules or expectations. It finds its way into our hearts, creating a connection that surpasses boundaries and stands the test of time.

As our connection deepened, Louie and I became inseparable. Our journey together unfolded with a delightful rhythm. Double dates, picnics, and Broadway shows became the backdrop to our growing romance. Louie's playful demeanor and infectious laughter made every moment memorable. A chance encounter where a stranger who mistook him for Vin Diesel, added a touch of humor to our story, highlighting Louie's larger-than-life personality. Our understanding of each other deepened as Louie shared his darker moments. He became a source of strength and comfort, a partner with whom I could face life's challenges. He was not just a brushstroke in the canvas of my life but a vibrant palette that added hues of joy, love, and resilience. Our love story truly embodied against all odds, our connection thrived, and our journey stood as a reminder that love unfolds in its own time. My first husband, my anchor through life's storms, the embodiment of protection and fierce love, was abruptly taken away, leaving me adrift in a sea of unimaginable grief. Our love story had been a sanctuary of dreams, laughter, and shared joy. In this lifetime, however, I never envisioned my journey weaving through the heartbreak of a tragedy that would forever change my existence.

3

Linda and James's Love Story

James was my friend, and he became my husband and my life partner. We lived in the same neighborhood. So, we saw each other on occasion just around the neighborhood. To me, he was just a regular guy on the block. I had seen him, but he did seem to be a bit older than I was. Then one day, I was standing at the bus stop on the way to work, and James spotted me, and he asked if I wanted a ride to work. I didn't really feel like waiting on the bus, so I said yes. While on the ride to work we talked and that's when I found out his age. I was 23 and he was 31. He also told me he was a Greyhound Bus Driver and from there our story began. During that short ride, he shared quite a bit about himself. I didn't tell him too much about myself because I didn't know him that well.

After that day, he seemed to make a point of passing by that bus stop to offer me a ride. It was kind of nice I thought, especially since it was a nice relief from the bus ride. He was so charming and nice looking too! I thought it was nice to have a guy friend, instead of always being with my girlfriends. We started seeing each other often, as he would ask me out for a date before I would exit his car, when he dropped me off at work. We would begin to frequent local parks, restaurants, and enjoy the drive-in movie theaters. He was a lot of fun, and so we became very good friends. I could see that he was very kind just by the way he spoke, by the things he did for me and others, and by the things he said.

After a couple of years of serious dating, James asked me to marry him, and we moved in together. His kindness and affection swept me off my feet and I felt a strong feeling in my heart for James. I was really falling in love with him. We got married after three years of dating, on April 20, 1979.

I had a 6-year-old daughter from a previous relationship, that he raised as his own. He was very loving in that way. That said a lot to me, and he made me very happy. God really sent this guy my way. I appreciated the many things he did for me, and he always included my family. He was kind to all of them. If they were in need of anything, he always offered to help. No matter who it was or what they needed.

In 1982, we had another bundle of joy. He was so happy to have another daughter!

I loved the way he cared for us.

He worked hard so we never wanted for anything. My husband still liked hanging out with his friends, which caused him to take time away from us. Most of the time that did not bother me because my family always had a lot of issues, so I always found myself helping them out of a situation. Sometimes I even had to take them into our home, and James was always agreeable and wanted to help. We had a lot of give and take in our relationship.

When James was out with his friends, he was the life of the party, and my family also loved him for that gift, as he extended his giving to them. He was a retired singer and musician when I met him, so that part of his life continued. He enjoyed being out and having a good time. His time in the entertainment world had been cut short after being drafted into the United States Army as a Sergeant.

He liked to party, and I did too but I was a mother now, so I felt it was my responsibility to stay home with the girls. Sometimes I felt he put his party time ahead of us, but then we decided that it was time to put this issue on the table and talk about it, until we could settle it. I had issues with control, and he had issues with partying but through meetings and therapy, we made adjustments. It was not an easy rode, but ultimately with the help of God we learned to communicate effectively and compromise.

I am so glad we took time to communicate and work things out together. That fact certainly saved our marriage and our love for one another. Now we could see clearly, and it was because of clear communication, but we both had to agree to work at it, and we did. When we did our part, God did the rest.

We both loved to travel and host family gatherings, and if there was anything anyone needed in our family, they knew we were always there to help. Sometimes this could put a strain on things, but as I said we found that talking about it would bring about the best results. My husband was a very caring person, he loved his family and friends. He was my "Jim-bo" and I loved him for that, and of course a few other reasons.

Although I was his help mate, he always helped me significantly in so many areas of my life, and he even assisted me tremendously with my parents and siblings through their illnesses and life struggles. He never questioned why I needed to help them, he just always made himself available and willing to be there to help. As I write these words, I truly realize that he was my rock, my superhero, because he was so dependable.

Even though my husband grew up in church he strayed away from the ways of the Lord. However, I knew God had been tugging at his heart and God was always with him. After his retirement he went back to church full time and was very active until the very end of his life. He joined CAG and became a part of the transportation ministry. He was faithful to that.

4

Bev and Lee's Love Story

When I met Lee as a young man, he was part of a close community and he had several very close friends such as Rand S, Rich C, Mark H, and Tally G, to name a few. Lee was the "Man" on his block. He wore white tee shirts all the time, what they call wife beaters now. He had thick nappy hair, which always had a pick stuck in it. I don't even know how later in our lifetime; he convinced me to wear an afro on my wedding day. I guess it was my love for him. (Thank God for the change, because later in his life, he wore expensive suits, he had a clean haircut, and his nails always manicured, better than mine.)

Falling in love was still a little new to me, I did not have much experience in that area, as I only had one real boyfriend before him. I think maybe I liked a couple of guys, but no one did I just love. I had secret crushes in high school, but absolutely nothing became of them. Then I seriously liked a couple of guys in college, they were tall, sweet, and good looking, except they both had girlfriends, and those girlfriends were my friends. So, I had to keep my distance and hands off, for the most part. I always had great religion/life conversations with them. I remember those college days, sitting in the cafeteria, surrounded by a group of guys who were not interested in me, but they enjoyed my religious world view conversations, as it always held their attention and took up their time until class or their girlfriends showed up. They were intrigued by it. Those times being a virgin was not bragged about, just meant to some that you were lame and not part of the popular in crowd. Most knew my status and I guess they were amazed by it, or maybe they were just thinking how that could relieve me of it.

You might say Lee was seemingly the leader of his group. In his spare time, he enjoyed playing cards, cee-lo, and pool. He liked to spend time with his friends after school and together, the boys landed their first jobs as Youth Workers, at the community center in the Bed/Stuy area where I was the director. That was where we first met.

I Got the Job!

My aunt Ruth was the coordinator of the program and in charge of her block association. So, the boys from the block were preferred. (Especially if the parents were part of the association.) It was because of her and her board of directors, that after being interviewed (although I was an outsider, but was qualified), that I got the job as "Youth Director." I, in turn, would have to interview for my staff, first position, "Youth Worker," and there were only two positions. Everyone knew that I was not from that block and the niece of Ms. Ruth, but I was qualified and nice, so they let it ride.

I interviewed with the board of directors; my two candidates and they were hired. Lee was less talkative than his friend Richard, but they both made the cut. I think Lee had his sights on me from then. I had to hire 8 other youth to work under them and after all interviews were over, I knew I had my work cut out for me. I had to train 50 other teenagers (first time having a job) to help the "Youth team." We would be responsible for 200 children, and nothing could happen to them.

I was more mature for my age, which was 20 and Lee was very mature (street wise) for his age of 17. Of course, since I was the new kid on the block (and fresh meat, and I mean that figuratively), Lee seemed to have first dibs. My dad let me reside at my aunt's house which was across the street from the community center and across the street from where Lee lived. Lee would walk me home from work, and he always did my bidding. I felt very protected by him, because he was tall and strong, and he seemed very nice. Besides Brooklyn was a little scary for me.

Lee's Hero Day

We had taken the children from the center on a field trip. I don't remember how many, but it was a lot. It involved taking the subway trains, and escalators. Thank God this was not a trip to the beach. On the way home from the trip, everyone was tired, but alert and one of our small children got his shoe or shoelace caught in the escalator and he fell. Unfortunately, this was at the top of rush hour in Brooklyn. When the little boy fell, it caused his clothes and his skin to get caught in the escalator, as he was close to the top. Lee, who was at the top of the escalator, saw what was happening. Grown adults began tripping over the young boy and falling on top of him. This young very small frail child could have been trampled to death, because the escalator was still moving. Lee jumped into action, actually picking up the adults and throwing them to the side and off the young child until he could reach him and pull him up. Unfortunately, the escalator tore into some of his skin. He had to go to the hospital for care. This accident could have been way worse if Lee had not gone into action as quickly as he did. He actually saved this little one's life. This little boy became our baby from then (Lam), and he would be that for some years. (This was a little boy who lived on the block and who was neglected by his mother but cared for by his very mature, dedicated nine-year-old sister.)

We Started Hanging Out

Lee was a gentleman, and I was a lady. He got to know me pretty quickly as he got permission to come over and stand in the yard and talk to me. My aunt was the oldest sister of my dad, so she was watchful, and not forgetting, she was a PK (preacher's kid). Sometimes I came outside, other times we would talk from the window until dark. He told me that all of his other girlfriends were way older than him, some he said were grown women. They probably contributed to some of his delinquencies.

Once Lee met me, I was not only his supervisor, but I would later become his wife, and his lifelong friend. That fact does not mean he didn't have other girlfriends, but he tried to keep me close. This journey would take us through a courtship and marriage times two, with some good and bad times, and a friendship that lasted fifty plus years, at the time of this writing.

A Bit of Jealousy

Lee tried to act so mature. One thing about him though, was that he was very jealous. He didn't want anyone talking to me. It was cute for a moment but got annoying to me quickly. I was new to the game, but I knew I was nobody's personal possession. After my summer job was over, Lee and I found a way to see each other on the low-low, because I really was still not allowed to date. (Remember, I was 20 years old.) Dating was the conversation that I never had with my dad who had been raising me. My dad was very protective, and I guess he thought this was the best way to protect me. The older I got, I kind of agreed. However, I believe I would have done the right thing as a young adult, because my home training was pretty solid. He was an awesome father, just very, very strict. Once I got out into the world I understood his reasoning. What he instilled in me, did not get into everyone else.

When I left home at 21, Lee got to see me with permission, at my aunt's house in Queens. Lee and I dated for a while, sitting on the stoop, or taking short walks to the neighborhood park. My aunt allowed me more privileges, so we started going to the movies, going to Coney Island, and a few other places. I am very thankful to my aunt and uncle for trusting me and allowing me to spread my wings. They treated me like a daughter. I was very grateful. I didn't have to ask permission, I just had to let her know where I was going and for sure, I could not stay out all night. I don't remember the curfew, but I am sure it was reasonable, maybe 1:00 am. At the time of this writing, my uncle had passed away, but my aunt is 102 years young, and very much with it. My favorite cousin and I were the same age, and he went out with his friends, but most of them, if not all, were Christians. So, I guess he had a little more freedom, besides he was a male child. It was quite different for his younger sister.

Our Song Still Water

Every time Lee and I went to a house party (not many though, as I didn't like house parties because they were always dark). Growing up in Long Island, I was not really a fan of Brooklyn, especially not the section I grew up, even though I was born there. So, I needed to see who was in the place and also needed to know a clear way out, in case something jumped off. Even though house parties were really not my thing to do, whenever we entered a party, the DJ knew to play his song, which became our song, **"Still Water" by the four tops**, and we would dance like no one else was in the room but us. Sometimes they let us dance by ourselves. Everyone knew we were there, and I was his girl. I always liked that as a connection to a guy, it usually included a song.

On occasion, Lee started coming to Bethel Gospel Tabernacle church with me in Jamacia, and one night he went to the altar and gave his heart to the Lord. That made me happy, because we could be on the same page, for the most part. He also knew when he did that, it made me happy. I believe God really touched his heart and He drew Lee there with a couple of his friends. He did not have the kind of heart that was not impenetrable. It was a John D. Lawrence revival. He also attended a few Jackie McCullough revival services with me. Jesus got to him for sure and I knew it. I think Lee fell hard for me, even though he was a pretty tough guy, he had a soft heart. That made our relationship pretty easy for the most part. I guess we can't help the way we grow up and we don't have a say to what happens to us before the age of five.

Music Was a Connection

While living in Queens, I got swindled by a couple of people because I was kind and naive, and now I was angry and from that point I didn't want to have anything to do with people, including Lee, but he was not having that. I think we got into this song, by **Michael Jackson (the Jackson Five), "Never can say goodbye,"** and we stayed together through my pain and anger, but it made me a little more aware of people. He tried to help in his own way. It was a hard time for me, because I was a cop's daughter, and I should have known better, but I learned.

Soon I got my own apartment downtown, around the corner from where I was going to start attending nursing school. I was pretty brave then, because I did that by myself. I got to see the world up close, and it was scary, but I had God and my protector Lee, who helped me to navigate the world and some of the people in it. I remember we used to take walks on Fulton Street, where the ladies of the evening could be seen. I was amazed to see them and their handlers in real life. Lee was cool and would always try to redirect my line of sight, telling me not to stare. LOL. I had only seen that kind of thing in the movies. It amazed me. Some movies we went to see were, Shaft, Super fly, Cleopatra Jones, Foxy Brown, and Hit Man, to name a few. I guess as a teenager, I really didn't miss too much, as the movies would not have been high on my agenda, mainly because they were always dark. I didn't like dark.

The Marine's—A Way Out

Lee had vision and asserted his blackness and wanted to exert his manhood by establishing his place in society and in life. He joined the military, and that certainly gave him more than he expected but even through the rough times, he hung in there. It opened his eyes somewhat, to what the world would be like and how people could treat you, and you'd have to stand up and take it or not. I know the military made Lee focused and stronger mentally. He was tough but sensitive. There were a few guys, I mean men that tried to talk to me, and they tried flaunting their good paying jobs in my face, but I was in love. Besides my dad taught me never to be swayed by money. THINK . . . That a person's integrity was more important than money and status.

His One True Love

In 1972 Lee wrote in one of his letters to me, that "if God made anyone better than me, He kept them for Himself." This was so sweet, and for that matter, men don't write that way too much anymore. Lee also wrote that I was really his first true love. I really didn't remember him ever telling me that. I always figured that if you had a girlfriend, that you probably were in love. I guess that's not a true fact of life.

Before he left for boot camp, I gave him a going away party, his cousin came, and his cousin invited my brother. Of course, at the time I didn't really know either one of them.

Reunited

I had not seen my brother since I was about 7 years old (he was not my father's son), so I didn't know him at first sight. It was his cousin and my older brother, Freddy, who were C-mates, that brought about the reunion with my birth mom and the siblings I never knew I had. Besides, it was dark at the party. Lee was shocked and suspicious that I was even related to my brother Freddy (who was very good looking and a guy from the streets), but God knows everything, and it was God that orchestrated this reunion. God knows the end at the beginning. I had reunited with my older brothers, Freddie and Bobby, who had a serious reputation in Brooklyn, so the word was already out, and no one would dare mess with me because I was the "good little sister" of Big Fred.

My brother Freddy was really handsome, and he was so

funny. LOL. I loved him so much and he loved me, but he did scary street things. My brother may have given me that title because I didn't grow up in the hood and he knew my Caribbean Brooklyn born father.

I remember my brother Fred telling his acquaintances not to talk to me and he would blink his eyes as if he was going to spaz out if they even looked in my direction. I'm not sure my brother could fight physically, but he had means of eliminating any foes. My brother Freddie was absolutely beautiful inside too, and so funny. LOL.

I felt myself really liking Lee, even though he was a little possessive. (I knew I didn't have to accept that behavior, but I did, because I didn't have much dating experience, and I let my heart take charge.)

The Accident

Once it caused us a very serious problem, almost deadly. He was so angry, because I was with my mom looking for my little sister, which he thought put me in a dangerous position. When he got behind the wheel of my car, he drove so fast down Howard Avenue that we got into a very bad accident. People had to take me and him out of the car, and they laid me on the ground. I had a lot of books and items in the car, but nobody really messed with the contents of the car, because someone in the crowd made note that I was Freddie's little sister. At that point they protected my stuff and me, until the ambulance and police arrived. Fred had a reputation in Bed/Stuy. Well, we survived that incident.

Not only would I, in time, get to help my two little sisters, but down the road, my sisters would birth two angels that would become part of my life (KK & Destiny).

Lee remained in the service, and when he eventually came home on leave, he wanted to move in. We didn't like being apart from each other so he came home as often as he could after boot camp. He would always call me to tell me how many days before he was home. Sometimes he would say, for example, "two days and a wake up." I loved to hear that phrase. It kept me connected with anticipation for his visit. Of course, I had to share his short weekend visit with his family.

We Were Going to Get Married

I started going to a few churches in Brooklyn, when I could not get to Queens. When Lee was home, he came with me. Churches like Bible Way (Pastor Hughie Rodgers) and Pilgrim (Bishop Roy E. Brown). We knew that living together could not be done so we decided to get married to make that part okay, besides we loved each other, he was still in the service, and we believed we would be together forever. Besides and more importantly, my father could not even think that some guy was living with me. LOL.

He Was My Protector

I felt safe in a scary world, in which I was navigating alone for a time, but at times protected with Lee. My brothers were a little too wild for me. They were interesting and so were their friends, but too much for me. I inserted myself into their lives on occasion, but it was a bit much more than I could handle, as grown as I thought I was. It was a little too dangerous and I was far from cool. When Lee was home, we were always together, when he wasn't visiting his mom and siblings. We would take his little brother to hang out with us a lot. We acted like he was our son and one of my sisters was my daughter. I guess we thought we were really grown. It was through Lee, that I was reunited with my birth Mother again. That part kept me busy with my mom, sisters, and nieces. My sisters and nieces sort of stayed with me a lot and we were always shopping. I felt like they were my little kids.

It was not long after that I reunited with my dad, because I did not leave home in a proper way. He got to meet Lee, and I suppose he liked him, but I don't really think anyone would have been good enough for his daughter. I'm sure once he knew about Lee, he pulled his yellow sheet and totally investigated him.

My dad played the game, and he let me know he was playing the game. Lee was nervous around him, but he got comfortable enough to ask him for my hand in marriage, even though we were already secretly married so I'm glad my dad said "yes." What would we have done if he said NO? I remember they went out and played a couple of games of handball together. Very interesting. My dad was pretty cool, even if I didn't think that all my life. He was sooooooooo strict. Now I know, strict was good for me. We had gotten married six months before my public wedding. He knew that was the only way to go.

Another Wedding Day

We had a beautiful wedding, which my dad paid for and he acted like the crazy but smooth father of the bride. We wanted one of the ladies from the church to sing one of our songs, **"You and I"** by Stevie Wonder, but she thought it was too secular and sang "Our Father." However, after the wedding with smiling so much, taking pictures, and talking, that I didn't even get to eat my food. I was exhausted. Thank God my caterer (Mr. Adams Sr.) fed us a meal the week before, it was our taste testing of the wedding meal, also because he knew brides didn't always get to eat their food properly at their wedding reception. Lee and I really went to sleep that night after the reception. LOL. After riding around a few hours looking for a hotel with a vacancy, guess we didn't plan that detail, and that's the only thing we did that night. We were really just kids in grown up bodies. I'm smiling writing this because it's a special memory, we were truly exhausted. We almost gave up looking for a hotel, we probably ate some fast food, protected the top of our wedding cake in the car, because I think my dad held our wedding gifts. Then we made out in the car. lol. We were legal times two.

We were happy and in love and started our life in Brooklyn, New York, but he was still in the service. So, I was mostly at the apartment alone. Being married was certainly a new experience for me. I only think I felt grown, making dinner for two, doing a man's laundry with mine, but I had so many other things on my plate. School being a major issue. I loved nursing, but the process was a bit overwhelming. I'm glad my dad taught me about money, but not really credit cards. I learned about that the hard way. Lee was sending me money anyway, and I knew how to budget. I finally moved into one of my father's brownstone houses because my rent at the apartment went up $15.00 from $150.00. LOL.

Having a Baby

I got pregnant as Lee was always coming home on leave. I was still working at the center while I was going to school. My aunt didn't believe my due date because I was so huge. I was huge because I loved to eat good food. Every time I was pregnant, I would say "there's a reason for the season," so I would eat for two. However, I made my due date, even maybe a week late. I had my first baby while living in Brooklyn, and Lee came home for her birth. We had gone to Lamaze classes and had a private doctor. However, when it was time for the delivery, my private doctor went down for coffee and missed the delivery. Lamaze wasn't working for me either. All that breathing stuff was out the window when the rubber hit the road. I think I bit Lee once when he put his hand on my shoulder and told me to relax and breathe. It is hilarious when I think about it now.

Lee's trip home was also very interesting, as he was determined to get home for our baby's birth. (At one point on his trip, he missed a flight and had to take a taxicab from one state to another and gave the cab driver a personal check. Amazing determination. Luckily, he was in uniform.)

The day we brought the baby home, when we got to the

car outside of the hospital, my dad tried to take the baby from the nurse, but the nurse said she had to give the baby to the mother. When we got to the house, my dad accompanied us and took the baby from me out of the car. Then I guess Lee got to hold her and bring her into the house. My dad was hilarious. Lee was kind of scared to hold the baby anyway, but he was so gentle with her, I guess he was scared he would drop her. After my daughter was home, Lee went back to his base and my dad started hanging out with me, and we became even closer. Lee was still in the service and not home often.

My dad and I would spend time together in the mornings drinking hot water and chatting about life. I enjoyed our talks now, as a young woman. I could sit now, not like when I was a kid and had to stand at attention and listen to his lectures, which I couldn't wait to end. The only thing I wish would have happened at this point, was that my father could have shared more with me than he did. He probably still viewed me as "his little girl," and maybe he didn't want to recognize that I was growing up. He probably needed to talk to me about real people and the evil that was in this world, which was even closer to home, even as close as family. That might have been the only thing he did not really prepare me for, or maybe I just didn't really listen well. As most young people don't really listen and take heed to the entire story but only focus on what is going on in their own head at the time. So, I will take responsibility for that part, because my dad really did try to prepare his children for life. Now I wish I could have those talks again, and I probably would have asked more questions. Especially about his relationship with my mom. I needed to know a little bit more about his life.

Knowing I did not want to raise my baby in Brooklyn, I asked if we could buy our family home in Long Island. He agreed. I guess since he was spending a lot of time in Brooklyn anyway. I didn't realize he was staying in Brooklyn most of the time and in the upstairs apartment. He kept that part secret from me, so I guess in a way he was still watching over me. My dad was so helpful to me while I was in school. Like when I had my first daughter, Kimberly, he would watch her some days while I was in hospital training. I took her to school for lectures, at times. Sometimes he acted like he was the parent. When I took her out, he would tell me how to dress her, like he was the mother. However, I never gave him a disrespectful response to his help. He did buy a lot of things for us, and he was a very proud grandfather. He brought Kimberly her first real baby carriage, not a stroller. It was burgundy and beautiful. I took a lot of walks with her, I felt very special, like rich people.

He brought us a washing machine so that I wouldn't have to go to the laundromat. Then he put a clothesline in my backyard so I could hang the clothes to dry. I loved that. My dad was so funny, however not as funny as the day I went into labor. I was glad we were friends again, that was a nice feeling. It is a feeling I will cherish for a lifetime. Sometimes good parents seem to be very hard on their children, and the children don't realize that good parents only want the best for them. Many parents want you to miss the steps that will have you come crashing down into complete failure and they don't want you to make mistakes that could cost you irreputable damage, even your very life. But sometimes experience is necessary and maybe quite possibly, so is failing and falling, hopefully not down to the gutter. I can add, if you fall down, get back up again as quickly as you can. Hopefully if someone sees you down, they will help you back up. That's the power of love, family and community.

Sad Day

Then suddenly, and without warning, my dad passed away. Some lady called me and called for an ambulance, and they brought my dad from upstairs in that brownstone building. I was hysterical. Right now, I can't remember what I did with my baby, but I'm glad I was home. Lee came home again as I was inconsolable because in four days, my dad passed away.

Lee was home a lot, and during that week, I conceived my second child, Kelly. I did not handle my dad's death well and then Lee came home for good. He supported me at my graduation, as it was 5 months after my dad died. I remember that my instructors and my classmates had to encourage me to continue to complete my degree. I wanted to quit, because I did not want to become like some of the nurses I met on my journey, nor did I want to work in some of the hospitals that I had trained. I missed my dad, so I didn't care who else was there at graduation. In all of my graduation pictures you will see the bags under my eyes from crying during the entire ceremony. I cried every day about the loss of my dad. I could be simply washing dishes, cleaning the house and would break out crying uncontrollably. After Lee did his time in the service he returned home, due to his mother being ill, my dad passing, we just had a lot going on. Then he was honorably discharged.

We Were in Love—Life Was Good

Lee loved the holidays, especially Thanksgiving and Christmas. He always participated in cooking as he said he had learned all that in the military, and even though he made a lot of mess in the kitchen, I was happy for the help. As a couple, life was good, but it became somewhat of a struggle because we should have talked more about our expectations in marriage, we were young, I mean he was young, and we had a lot more responsibility and probably didn't have all the tools to deal with those extra responsibilities, or the proper support, family/community, my dad, that we needed for a successful marriage. I was quiet, but Lee had a temper. That was not good for us. Thank God we didn't fight or argue in front of our children. Like I said we were still learning.

We went on a real honeymoon after our third child was born. We enjoyed the Poconos, and we took the baby because she was sick and we didn't want to leave her home with my young sister, who was like my daughter, and my other children.

I may have not been a good wife after he was discharged, because I was so very depressed. I was juggling a lot, as I inserted my new family into that part of my new life with my husband. He was young, so that may have been a lot of stress on him also. I may not have looked depressed or manifested out loud symptoms, I internalized my pain and only those close could feel it. I think Lee could feel it. He visited his mom a lot. I thought he spent too much time away from home doing whatever, I may just have been a lot for him. We had a lot of growing up to do. Lee did his best and tried to be a good father and he was funny too. He still acted like if he picked up the babies, they would break. So, he was very gentle with the girls, and that included the discipline part, so he left most things up to me and he went to work.

Lee was still young, but he had to grow up fast for real now. The party was over, we both had to live a grown-up life. When we moved to Long Island, he brought our growing family a brand-new blue station wagon. He became part of Amityville Gospel Tabernacle and started working at the post office. He would still check on his mother and siblings regularly, because they were still a close-knit family. He tried to be the man in our family, even though he didn't see a lot of examples, and I was a lot to deal with, major because I saw a very strong example of a man and a father. I wasn't crazy, just maybe set in certain ways. We separated then divorced after thirteen years, but our love story did not end there. We were still deeply connected and still on a journey that was complicated.

Lee Had a New Level Job

Lee had a new job working for the government now. His office was at 26 Federal Plaza. He was there until two weeks before September 11, when he was transferred a short distance away. He had not completely moved all of his papers from that location when that deadly situation occurred. God was certainly faithful. He could have lost his life, as some of his friends and co-workers did on the fateful day.

I Didn't Know That

Today I got a visit
from your middle child.
She shared something that
you told her many years ago.

It touched my heart,
however, there is not much
I can do about it now,
because I didn't know.
I was the one who held your heart.

I knew we had a love between us,
Some things you just know for sure.
However, when our way got shaken
and things went awry,
our blue skies faded,
*for a season, the **"Still Water"** went dry.*
The story line became blurred,
*Then it was no longer **"You and I."***

But I will always have a love for you.
My first husband, twice married,
the father of three of my daughters,

and two more almost,
my once lover and my forever friend.

As I look back to those beautiful
days when we struggled together,
we slept with our baby on a twin bed,
at least we were together,
but then somehow, we lost our way.

Then we traveled down a different
path and our hearts got confused.
However, when the dust settled,
and the storms stopped blowing,
we wiped our eyes,
because we could see clearly,
from our **16th floor studio** *view.*

That our love for each other
had fallen in a distant muddy field,
Still watered by the dreams of our children.
They carefully held on to a hope
that one day the sun
would shine on our hearts, again.
That our hearts would be mended
together, after a while and forever.

I just didn't know I really had
your heart, and that your first

real love began with me.
Even though you said,
I was one in a million
I was the first, the last,
your everything. *Then I realized,*
things changed, people change,
but I'm glad we once fell in love.

Now this year of 2024
I know if you could,
you would be witty and
still laugh at your own jokes.

If you could, I know you would
just remember the time,
precious times we held hands
on the streets of Brooklyn.
We went to the movies, to the parks,
on boardwalks and on Coney Island,
where I felt safe and protected by you.

Of course, you were a brave Marine,
entering that branch of service,
too young to know how many ways,
it would change your life forever,
good and then horribly bad.

However, I am so proud of you
because you were determined to
take your life of service to new heights,
then to a new level.
You always presented as a tough guy,
which is why you were chosen
to guard the President.

So, I would only just smile, and I would try
to chase your sickness, your sadness,
and move heaven to chase your pain away.
*Because there was a **Ribbon in the Sky***
for our love.

I pray you will always know in your heart,
my love was your love. No person could
ever change that, and I would thank you
for the precious gifts you gave me.

It's been 50 years—almost a lifetime.

A friend once told me, there will always
be one girl that will hold a man's heart.
But . . .
You said, "when a man loves a woman"
and at the time,

*I didn't know **"how deep was this love"***
Then you wrote in a letter,
"If God made anyone better,
He kept them for Himself."

That "one" girl, that will hold a man's heart,
which it is a great responsibility,
I didn't know . . .
I just didn't know . . . that girl was me.
And now, still . . . I cry. ***BJA***
11/30/24
But now " for Pete's sake"
his love and friendship blocked
the memories of
Our yesterday's love

And then I watched Luther's video
"Can I Take You Out Tonight"
his movement, his lips, his teeth,
his face, his skin color, and did you know?
just think
I've physically touched you both.

Your resemblance to him, makes me
take a second look. However, the song
unblocked my memories of you
It unlocked my feelings for you.

So, I watched it many times.
Then I smiled,

Now I can omit the jealousy from you
I can forget the sadness about you and
I can forgive the violence and heartbreak from you
So now, I can clearly remember the love from you

I can clearly remember the dances with you,
Wish we could dance, I would still dance with you
When sophisticated innocence met street smart,
only realized we needed each other to grow up.
I'm still holding your heart for you.
And now . . . Still I smile. **BJA**

5

Dorothy and Caselle's Love Story

How We Met

"Noooooooooo! Don't do that! I am so scared!!!" This is what I told my date standing beside me looking out the restaurant window as the snow continued to pile high. We were having dinner at a hilltop restaurant in Tulsa, Oklahoma. The ice storm had come suddenly and before we knew it, we were trapped atop the hill along with the other patrons and facing an incredibly slick ride to the street below. Restaurant employees went down the hill and blocked traffic as each patron took their turn driving out the iced-over parking lot and down the dangerous path to the road below. Most lost control. Earlier, I told myself I'd drive my car to the restaurant so if this "date" didn't work out, I'd have a way home. Now, I was terrified to drive my own car! How did I get myself into this situation? If I was to date at all, it was to be a minister. Caselle (that was his name) said he'd drive, but I didn't trust him. Honestly, he was a little wacky! I'd met him a couple of months before. I worked as an accountant for Oral Roberts Ministries and the first day we met he said the Lord told him I was not going to lose my job. He said everyone around me was going to lose theirs, but I would leave my job when I wanted to.

Caselle was a 30-year-old theology student moving into one of the apartments owned by the ministry. He had travelled from Memphis. It was my job to see that students paid the rent or had arranged for payment before they were issued keys. He had no money and no place to stay. He became a frustration from Day 1. I had seen it a hundred times . . . people coming to ORU with no money.

This was a bad time for the ministry. President Roberts had made the statement that God was going to "take him home" if he didn't raise a certain amount of money. The ministry had already lost the law school and was about to lose the City of Faith. It was all over the national media. The ministry had become a mockery. Donations were drying up and staff was being let go. What was generally unknown was how many people (and their families) this ministry was taking care of for free because they had travelled across the country (and the world) to come to ORU because they believed in "seed faith," one of this ministry's founding principles. ORU fed and housed them, most times never getting any financial return. I saw Caselle as one of these people. Miraculously, no matter how many deadlines I imposed on him, he obtained favor from my superiors and remained in his apartment. I found him very handsome, but he simply got on my nerves.

We almost got into a heated confrontation when he called my office asking what I considered a ridiculous question. A member of my staff intervened, asking him to come to my office after closing time to discuss our issues. She told him I requested the meeting and at the same time told me he requested the meeting with me to iron out our problems. She told me later that she thought we'd make a perfect couple. We did iron out those issues and learned we had a lot in common. He eventually invited me to lunch (to the student cafeteria!!!) and later to this hilltop restaurant for dinner. I knew I was supposed to marry a minister, but he'd never mentioned anything to me about being in the ministry nor was this date considered anything more than friendship.

The more I saw the weather getting worse and seeing what a predicament I'd gotten myself into, I began to verbally lash out at him and myself, telling him that I wasn't supposed to be dating anyone and that I was supposed to marry a minister. I told him that was the reason we were in this trouble now. Caselle calmed me down, got in the car and drove us down the hill safely. He didn't even raise his voice. I was completely embarrassed. To my surprise, he said, "Don't worry. I am an ordained elder in the Church of God in Christ. I have my ministerial license and ordination papers." He even had his own ministry, Fire of New Azusa. I asked why he never mentioned it. He said it never came up.

Well . . . the rest is history. We met in January and married in October. We had 3 children and stayed married 35 years. We never even kissed before our wedding day. I lost him a little over a year ago and I miss him terribly. By the way, he wasn't a false prophet either. Everyone in my department at ORU lost their jobs, including my boss, except the director of student housing, the maintenance supervisor and yours truly!!

The scripture given above was my husband's favorite! We lived it every day, realizing we could not even stay married in our own strength and power. We were like oil and water. Marriage is not for the weak or the selfish. It is not even a 50-50 partnership! Many times, we were happily married but also many times we were unhappily married. But we were STILL married, and we were committed to stay that way . . . by His Spirit! I thank God for the time He gave me with Elder Caselle Corintheus Knox III. It was truly a wild ride!! Our love and friendship remained strong, even through some difficult times, and for that I am thankful.

6

Jacque and Robert's (Bob's) Love Story

It all started in the Second Semester of Sophomore Year at the University of Florida. My freshman year, I went steady with a young man in a fraternity, but the relationship just wasn't meant to be and we broke up at the beginning of my sophomore year. Following the breakup, I had a lot of fun dating several young men, one of which was Bob. I met Bob through some mutual friends. I would often see him in the Campus cafeteria having lunch with 3 of his close friends, 2 of which he had gone to Gainesville High School with since they all grew up in Gainesville. I would be sitting at a table by myself since most of my friends ate a little later than I did. Bob would come over and speak to me and after a few weeks, asked me if I would like to join their table, which I did and enjoyed their company. A couple of months later, my dorm had an open House, and only then could men come upstairs and see the rooms of friends, Bob had been visiting our mutual friend upstairs when I ran into him in the hallway and invited him to come by my room.

Even though the dorm had a rule for no alcoholic beverages

in the dorm, I had a bottle of rum hidden in the bottom of my closet and I offered to spike Bob's punch that he had gotten downstairs with the refreshments, and he accepted. We started dating soon after that and he always told people that "The Big City Girl" (I grew up in Miami) took advantage of the "Small Town Boy." He grew up in small towns including Gainesville (with the drink), and that's how we got together. I don't think that was the only reason we dated for 2½ years and were married for 59 years, but he enjoyed telling the story. He also liked to play Bridge with his buddies. Before dating Bob, I didn't play Bridge, but soon learned as his buddies didn't appreciate me sitting in his lap while they were planning cards.

After we both graduated, we got married on August 11, 1963. As we were starting to plan our wedding, Bob thought we would be married by a Justice of the Peace like his parents had. But I said "Oh No" we can visit any church you wish until we find one we both like and we will get married there. We found a lovely Mission Lutheran Church that we both loved and got married in the University Lutheran Church because the Mission church hadn't built their church yet and were still meeting in a school auditorium.

A month after we were married, we packed all of our belongings, including wedding presents and took off for Newport, R. I. There Bob attended Navy Officer Training School and Naval Justice School. While Bob was at Navy OCS he had to live on base during the week, so I had a room in a lovely historic mansion by the sea, with kitchen privileges in the basement. Bob would come home on the weekends. A friend from our church in Gainesville FL, knew the owners and recommended that we stay there. The owners were very good to us and also went to the Lutheran Church.

We made several trips on the weekends around New England as we both loved to travel and see new places. We decided as we left Newport, our last New England trip would be to Niagara Falls. It was absolutely gorgeous and breath takingly beautiful. We left Niagara Falls and drove to Ohio to visit some of Bob's relatives and then onto Gainesville, Florida where I stayed with our families for about 3 months while Bob flew over to the Western Pacific to meet the ship. He would be on for his first tour of duty. The ship's home port was San Diego.

Bob's military career required many adjustments on both of us. We rose to the occasion in many instances. We had our first daughter in San Diego, and our second in Maryland while he was stationed at the Washington Navy Yard. To add to our many adjustments, his third duty station was in Saigon for 13 months working on Building projects around South Vietnam. The girls and I stayed in Gainesville, Florida near family. Bob and I got to meet in Hawaii for R and R which was wonderful for both of us to have some together time.

After he came home his last duty station was in Albany Georgia, at the Naval Air Station as Assistant Public Works Officer and we got to live in Navy Housing which was great for all of us. The Vietnam War was coming to an end and the Navy was downsizing. Bob was passed over for promotion and decided to get out of the Navy. He was absolutely crushed as he had planned to stay in the Navy until his retirement. It took quite a while for him to get over this disappointment.

At 16 my parents took me with them to Atlanta over New Years for a Sales Event as they were Traveling Salesmen. Being raised in Miami, I was absolutely amazed by Atlanta with its hills and trees and change of seasons. When we had to leave Albany in June of 1973, Bob agreed that we could move to Atlanta to please my longing desire to move there and because there were more job opportunities for him than in Gainesville Florida. Although we found a lovely house in Mableton, a western suburb of Atlanta, and it was also a wonderful church and schools for the girls. This was not an easy adjustment, as the construction industry was in a recession that year and jobs were not easy to get and to keep.

Finally in November God arranged a special interview for Bob, with a man named Rip, which was the answer to prayer. Bob accepted the job with Rip, and he mentored Bob to learn everything he needed to know about estimating Water and Wastewater Plants. Bob worked for Rip in Macon and Atlanta Georgia, and Montgomery Alabama. When the job in Montgomery came to an end, Bob secured a job as estimator with a company on the east side of Atlanta. We then lived in Tucker Georgia.

When we had lived in Mableton, a very important part of our lives took place at the Lutheran Church where we had joined. Our pastor and a few of our friends went to a Cursillo weekend. The Cursillo is to help Christians become Leaders. They came back from the weekend so excited that several of us could not wait to go. One of my lady friends and I were ready to make a weekend, but back then, the husbands had to go before the wives. My friend's husband had already gone, but Bob was not very interested. Unbeknown to me, my friend talked to Bob, and he agreed to go, mainly as a favor to me. Bob loved the weekend, and for the first time took Jesus for his personal Savior, even though he had been going to church with me since we were married and actively took part in many activities.

It was the beginning of a wonderful way of life for both of us to share in many ways. Not only were we both more active in church and as disciples, we were also very active working on Cursillo weekends and serving on the Secretariat of the Cursillo Movement in the Atlanta area.

After living in Atlanta for 4 years, we moved to Montgomery, Alabama for 6 years for Bob to be Rip's assistant in a new company there. While there we still were active in Cursillo and went to their meetings and also found out about Kairos, a Cursillo type weekend for Prisoners. Bob worked on a couple of Kairos weekends and then we moved back to Atlanta where Bob helped bring Kairos to the State of Georgia. God really enriched our lives everywhere we went. Bob and I continued to grow together on our Christian journey, learning to serve in many different ways.

7

Ja'nye and Pete's Love Story

Prologue

Ralph had many titles, and in no specific order, he became my husband, but first he was my childhood crush, my friend . . . my best friend, then my lover, and then father of two of my five birth children. Also, a stepfather to nine of my children and would have been a father to the two babies we lost in utero. Then he was a father to my two stepdaughters. It's all complicated, but you can read this story and then do the math if you wish. But as a teenager, I remember singing this song in church, titled "Walk on by faith each day." I would passionately sing that solo as if I knew all of the ramifications it would have on my entire life. I thought I would just let Jesus be my guide, and that would be easy. It wasn't as easy as my little heart would surmise.

He was a self-proclaimed narcissist, maniacal and egotistical in his behavior, which would sometimes peak through his charming-like sweet boy persona.

In the words of Luther, "I lived my life for him, and now

I'm left with me." Now heartbroken . . . Love was a journey and took time, but it was magical.

So, here's how my story begins:

First Encounters

When we first began it was unbelievable and ridiculous at the same time, because we were only 10 and 12 years old. I was that little fat girl, who wore thick glasses, so I don't know why he chose to pay any attention to me, except there were several boys on the prowl including my little brother, they were feeling their oats I guess, and only a few girls, including his sister, from whom to choose. In a way I felt lucky to be chosen, because he eventually turned out to be my soul mate. Later in life he would become my second husband. Ralph was his real name, but they called him Petie. He was a slim, brown skin cutie with wavy hair, sweet lips and a cute mold on his face.

We met at church. which at that time was a converted garage which was known as Amityville Gospel Tabernacle in the small town of Amityville, Long Island, NY. It was one of the churches the mother church "Bethel Gospel Tabernacle" had taken under their covering in 1959.

Petie's mom, Mary Elizabeth, was one of the founding members, as they began having bible study in their home and transitioned to a firehouse, then to the renovated garage at 8 Brefni Street. I started going there during the first couple months of 1960, with my dad, stepmom, brother and sister. Later my dad, Donald, would have a great impact on this church as it relates to their building fund projects. After a few weeks of attending Sunday school, we got to know the kids there a little better. During services, we always ended up sitting on the wooden benches, in the back rows. There were two electric heaters, one on either side of the church. It was also Petie's job to lite the heaters during the winter months. I liked watching him lite the heaters and I guess he felt important doing that job. (Side note: This is the same job my grandfather did as a young man in Brooklyn.)

Of course, back in that day we had no cell phones, which meant there was no texting, so we relied on pen and paper or just plain talking. All the kids were always passing notes to one another, hoping not to get caught. We also had to avoid getting caught talking to one another, so the only option was to pass notes. Petie would sort a flirt with me, but I paid him not much attention, as he winked at me and blew me kisses. I didn't like boys at the time, especially since where I came from in Brooklyn, the boys there were mean to me and would tease me and call me names.

One Sunday Petie Popped the Question . . .

After a few short weeks Petie passed me a note that said, *"will you go steady with me? check yes or no."* It wasn't even written on a whole sheet of paper. Just a neatly torn piece of paper, folded in squares. Since I really didn't understand all that, I would just check no.

(I'm now laughing out loud.) So, he did it a couple of Sundays. I really wish I had saved one of those notes. My Father was not always attending AGT with me and my siblings, only my stepmom, who was trying to get acquainted with the ladies of the church, so no one was making us be really attentive in church.

At some point I must have said yes, and by that time some of the kids were kind of paired up. We did what little kids did back then, and that was just chase each other around the church yard after service, until our parents were ready to go home. We would play tag, play hide and seek, especially so we could find the one we wanted to catch us. We didn't play outside much on Sundays because we had on our proper Sunday best clothes and shoes. We would dare not get dirty. We would sing that little song about sitting in the tree k-i-s-s-i-n-g. Now during church service, Petie would navigate himself to sit next to me. It was like quietly playing musical seating. I think he would sneak his arm around the area where I sat, and I guess I would simply smile. For sure his hand did not actually touch my shoulder. We also sang another song, which went like this, "first comes love, then comes marriage then comes _______ with a baby carriage." We pretty much had the concept, but not the process. (I heard some little kids still sing some of those songs.) None of it really made any sense to us. We probably didn't even know what we were talking about, more importantly we didn't really understand what any of it meant. You see, those were the days that even married people on television did not even share the same bed.

We were silly kids, and I don't think we ever kissed, well maybe we fumbled into one another, and maybe got a peak on the cheek. But as time went by it got a little more serious, well

I mean like real infatuation, because Petie and I saw each other in church at least four times a week. That's how many times people used to go to church back then. By now Petie had my attention, as he was way more streetwise than I was, because I was a little naive and not street wise at all.

Bible School Days—First Kiss

By the year 1962 (I was 12, he was 14), we were both attending Bible School at Bethel Bible Institute Extension class in Amityville. His mother was a registered nurse, a nursing instructor and BBI instructor, and she taught us both, along with Aunt Bea Caesar. There, Petie and I excelled in class, as we were both quick studies, and ahead of our classmates, so we were allowed, or maybe he volunteered us to go to the lower level to set up the refreshments for the class. That is what also got us our first kiss, I mean lip to lip. By this time, I think I was in love, because we got to kiss for real, well you know *"puppy love"* and as my Pastor's wife (Sis. Walker) would call it, saying that *"it was real to the puppy." Oh my, what a true statement.* She also told the young ladies to keep an aspirin between our knees and we would be sure not to have sex. She may **not** have said that "s" word, but it all meant to keep our legs closed. I didn't have to worry about that instruction, because I was too afraid of my Father to be that crazy, even though I did not have a clue. It was not even a thought in my mind. I'm glad I didn't understand all that adult stuff, because I really enjoyed my childhood. We played outside, played jump rope, hopscotch, and played on the swings. We fed the animals, rode our horse, tendered the crops. Life was pretty simple. No one really talked about that subject in those days, and it was not even implied. I'm almost glad it wasn't. So, if you didn't sneak and look in adult magazines, you didn't get to complicate your life with the adult stuff. We didn't understand that we would have enough time for that stuff. Thank God, "No social media." It also didn't take me long to find out that kissing didn't get one pregnant. I believe some adult implied that.

Young Preachers

I will add we both preached our first sermon at 13 years and 15 years. My sermon was titled "Trust and Obey" Pete's sermon was titled "Faith." When I was about 15 or 16, seeing Petie at church was probably one of the additional reasons I enjoyed going to church and went so faithfully. Then again, going to church wasn't really an option in my household. My dad came to our church a lot, but he mainly went to the mother church in Jamaica. He was part of the Full Gospel Hour Choir, under the direction of Sis. L. Figgins and they were on the radio, so I guess they were famous.

Fake Wedding and First Heartbreak

One Saturday after a youth meeting, Petie and I got play married in the church backyard, by Shirley, who was one of the girlfriends of my little brother. By the time I was 16, I was really going steady with Petie. Going steady means different things in today's world, but I was his girl. Like we would sit together in church and on every church bus outing, but one day, one of the church ladies (JSW) told my dad, and of course I was in big trouble. My dad confronted me asking me "where I was going with Petie?" I was shocked and was not prepared for that question. I had to tell my dad the whole detailed story because I believed he knew it anyway, he didn't usually ask a question he didn't already have the answer, and I was too scared to lie. I guess my dad understood what all that entailed, as he was once a NY cop and now a detective. I still did not, but kissing and holding hands was all most kids did in that day. I still could not go anywhere, like to the movies or parties like my friends could.

If truth be told, since I didn't attend the same school system as Petie, I just might have been his girl on the side or his church romance.

So, one day Petie made a choice to go with some other girl (one of my so-called friends, a church girl from my school). It was Petie's aunt that called me and told me to get right over to their house because another girl was there. She knew I liked him and at least I was a girl from her church, and really most all the girls in town went to one church or another. Some girls were really a little wayward. When I got to his house, Petie and I talked briefly and even though I BEGGED him not to, he said we were breaking up. But those are the breaks, and my first heartbreak. I mean I really begged him, oh my goodness, how silly of me and it was really an embarrassing moment. I was leaning on the side of a crib, which was in the room and the side fell down. If I had any pride at all, it was hurt, and I felt my heart was torn up. I was thinking how dumb of me, and to think I took a $3.00 taxicab there only to be dumped. If I can remember clearly, I don't think the breakup that day even seemed to bother Petie. It was a cold moment on a warm day.

My world felt crazy, and I had no one to talk to about what I was feeling. I was overcome with sadness, and it took a minute to get over it. Well maybe more than a minute. However, I'm glad we didn't have cell phones back in the day, as the situation could have been way worst. These are the things teens need to know, that they may go through, and things may even look quite dark, but they will get over it and time does go on. You don't have to take the opinion of other kids. God has you on a course for better. You don't have to consume the chatter or take the opinion of other kids, who know less than you do. The research has been done, how cell phones and the way they are used today have contributed to serious mental health issues and teen suicide, especially among girls. Things will get better as you go and grow, hopefully you learn like I did. The research has shown, how cell phones and the way they are used today are counterproductive. Researchers are calling this generation "an anxious and depressed generation." Things will get better. Life is a journey, and you must go the distance. One day is absolutely not the end of the road, nor the end of the world, **so don't jump.**

Petie came to church less and less, so we did not communicate, and I could not receive phone calls. (I didn't even ask my dad, because I knew the answer.) We still liked each other at a distance (I could tell by the look in his eye when we saw each other), however I was no longer his girl, so what difference did the look mean. Then when he was 18, he was off to the military and Viet Nam, and I figured that was the end of that.

Another Song—Words from James Ingram

Seems like yesterday.
We were still children with all our dreams, tomorrow
dreams.
Only yesterday you and I promised each other love.
forever love,
but now you're gone, and our dreams are scattered like the
leaves of fall,
wish I knew what happened to them all.
But no matter where I go or what I do,
there's always you.
Things change, people change,
growing up love can grow apart
we dreamed different dreams,
there I watched you drifting away, so far away.
but I believe that a love like ours
was somehow meant to be
And I will see the day when you come back to me.

Love Letters from Viet Nam

He finally wrote to me, as fate would have it (his mom or aunt brought the letters to church and gave them to me). I read them over and over, as I would envision something magically happening. **It did not.** His letters were so well written. I thought maybe he still liked me a little, because he would tell me he was lonely in Viet Nam and wanted to come home to me. He wasn't fighting over there because he worked in an office as an Administrative Specialist, but he went out on missions with the guys who were flying the planes. However, the war there affected him in many ways. He did not lose life or limb, but the way of war took something out of him. So, he came home with issues and demons from war. It hurt him mentally and held onto him for a long time. I prayed for him always, because I didn't want him to die.

Yet when he came home from the service, he brought someone with him. His mom stood up in church and said it was his wife. That's how she introduced the cute young, petit woman. His letters gave me no clue. I cried for days, and my heart was broken, again, thinking he was really married. I believed that it was over for us this time for real. You can't fight "wife," because that's kind of **final.**

When you love someone
And you've done all you can do,
then you set them free,
And if that love is true,
it will all come back to you.

Ran Away from home—Different Life

I left home at 21 (unrelated to that news) and moved to Queens, went to college, met another guy, fell in love and got married, then had two beautiful daughters, with my first real husband. I moved back to Long Island (1975), in my dad's house, and in the house in which I grew up. I still had friends there and I went back to my same church. I was comfortable with the familiar. Then I got a second phone call in 1977. It was him. The first call was when I was still living in Brooklyn. He had gotten my number from his mom. He called to say he had gotten in some trouble and wanted me to pray for him, and I did. He thanked me for checking on his mother. I figured that was that. It was a time I was going through a rough patch in my marriage, and also, I had third baby girl with my husband. Just a little time had passed after I had come home from the Poconos. I separated from my husband with a divorce pending.

The Second Phone Call

Then I got a second phone call in 1977. It was Petie, again. My sister Pat had come to live with me for a while, and at some point, she started hanging out with Petie. Every time she came home, I would try to get the 411 about Petie. Then one day Petie showed up at my door and this time he was looking for me. He still had the piece of my heart that he left with when he went into the military. When I opened the door, the look in his eyes, as he lifted them from looking at the ground, the sweet smile on his face, made my heart skip a few beats. I took a chance, and it took a minute, but then the rest is history.

What Was I Thinking

Time became a blur, I was still trying to work on my marriage, and sometimes not, I didn't know what I was doing. I was feeling grown, a college graduate, my dad was not there to help me make important decisions and talk me through my life situations or help me make important decisions. This was a choice I had to make by myself and then deal with the consequences. My dad and I had become very close from the time I had asked his forgiveness because of the way I left home. I actually had run away at 21. My friends were happily married and didn't need my drama. So, I kept my unstable life to myself. I did talk with God, but I'm not quite sure I was waiting on His answers. Sometimes God leaves you to your own crazy devices, and He does make a way of escape, if you want to take it. Then if you crash, God is always right there with loving kindness, to pick you up and hold you. His grace and mercy were always there for me. What God doesn't say, is "I told you so."

We Began Again—A Second Chance at Love— Twice in One Lifetime

It took some time, but it was about 1984 when *Petie and I began again.* I was about 34 and Petie was about 36. It was shortly after his marriage to another girl (GD), which lasted 62 days and the sudden death of his new steady girlfriend (Pat) from Suffolk State, with whom he had fallen in love. Not necessarily in that order but he was really devastated when Pat died suddenly, as they had visions of sharing a life together and having tall babies like themselves. I helped him through that time in his life and the funeral that followed was very hard for him. He was very sad, and he trusted me to be a sympathetic ear and shoulder as he grieved the woman he loved. That caused us to talk for hours. Petie trusted that I would listen to him talk about his love for another woman without having a jealous feeling. I was his friend, I could feel his heart and I cared about him.

This time was sad, magical and scary, all at the same time. Petie and I talked and talked mostly about his life, our parents, the good old days, some of his relationships, and we realized if nothing else, he and I would always be great friends. I was getting divorced and uncertain as to where my life would take me. I wasn't sure that I was ready for more grown-up decisions, and he was being so very sweet.

It was several days after Petie lost the girl with whom he was in love, that we met up. We were in deep conversation when something happened that I was not prepared for.

The Kiss

I didn't really think about it that night, but once he kissed me (for about 5 seconds), and this was the first time in seventeen years. I was an adult, so it felt different, and I was also surprised by it. Then he did it again, his face still wet with tears, this time he gently held my face to his, now, I was scared. I had to take control of myself and the situation, so I gently wiped the tears from his face with my hand, and backed away from his body, as if to change the atmospheric situation and catch my breath. I don't know what he was thinking, but only in my head I said, wow, because his second kiss was careful and long enough to confuse me. I didn't realize there was going to be more on the horizon, and I wasn't ready for anything else to happen, but there was *"Still"* a spark. Maybe he had waited 17 years to do that. Remember, we parted as teenagers, now we were full grown adults. However, he had respectfully held me close, releasing me but still touching my hand. He may just have been testing me the first time, or resting on my sympathetic heart, because I don't think this embrace was planned. He was really grieving the loss of his girl, and I was attentively listening because I felt his pain. Even though he was a man, I didn't think he could turn his emotions on and off that quickly. I would not have taken advantage of his grief and vulnerability; I thought it was simply a tender moment with an old friend.

I wiped his tears and convinced him that he needed to go to her wake/funeral. Fact was that they were a couple, and I felt his love for her. I offered to loan him money to buy a pair of black shoes for the services. He was not sure he could face it, but a few days later, I drove him there to say a final goodbye to his girl, his friend and left him. He looked good for the service in his all-black attire. I didn't think it would be proper to accompany him into the funeral home. So, I watched him walk across the parking lot and I just prayed he would be alright.

I guess he did okay that night as I didn't see or hear from him for about a week. One of my friends told me if you buy a man shoes, he will walk out of your life, however this guy was walking back into my heart and into my life. The great thing about Pete and I was that we always had great conversations, and boy could he talk. I wrote this about him later in our lifetime, that he truly had the "gift of gab." He knew a little about a lot of things because he was always reading. I was taken by his gift. Petie could even make you believe he was telling the truth about a subject and that whatever he said was really a fact, just by the way he said it. He once told me that if someone wanted to hurt him, they would not allow him to read. He was always reading, anything and everything.

Another Song—My Heart Belongs to You—
Peabo Bryson/Jim Brickman

Look at me now, thought I was near the end,
Then you came along when I needed a friend
And you made me love again,
somehow you found me,
Wrapped your love around me

Love Word Not in Our Vocabulary

We saw each other for dinner about a week after the funeral but we didn't really talk about it. However, I left a door open for him to talk about it if he wanted. He seemed to escape into deep thought even while looking at me. I could tell he was still deeply affected by his loss. We didn't talk about that kiss either. It was obvious to us that there was still a thing between us, so without going too deep, we would just have to see how this thing played out. I think we began a soft relationship, whatever that means. It was quite some time before we used the word love with each other. I think we were both being careful, respectful and scared. But I thought I found in him, something I needed. I think it was unfinished business. It was good that we had never been intimate in all of these years, as it would have complicated our friend relationship, and our friendship was the principal thing.

It didn't matter to me where he had been, or who he had loved because I was happy to have my dear friend back in my life again, and besides, my relationship with my husband was becoming more strained. So, it felt nice to have Petie pay attention to me, since my husband's attention seemed to have been drawn away. He was around just when I needed a friend, and he needed one too. So, we really had many great conversations and talked about so many subjects. I don't really know what he was thinking about that kiss, because we didn't actually talk about it, but I knew now, I had to tread cautiously.

Another friend of mine (RH) recently told me that men usually have one woman that holds his heart, no matter how many women he has been with, and I believe that I had Petie's heart, because he gave it to me to hold as a teenager.

I know Pete tasted a lot of flavors in his time on earth, and fact was, I would probably be the last one.

Something Crazy Happened—Petie Got Married

You heard what I just said. One day I was at my job when I got a disturbing phone call. I am drawing a blank now, but they called me to tell me Petie was a few blocks from me, and he was getting married at some girl's apartment. Maybe it was him calling to tell me he just got married, my memory is blocked. Not many people knew my job number. Of course, my heart hit the floor. I was confused as I could not imagine this was happening again. It was to someone I had no idea he was even hanging out with. Petie had at least three girls he would be with days at a time. He was not my boyfriend, and I wasn't keeping track of his whereabouts, so what could I say. However, it was a small town, so unless you were hiding, you might be spotted together in the grocery store or in the doctor's office, or just anywhere. I had too much going in my own life anyway. I knew some of the girls he hung with, and this was not one of them. However, I knew her. She (GD) was the cousin of my sister's good friend. This was shocking and again I was confused but I knew my life had to continue, but this was crazy. Had I missed the signs or was I just going completely blind. It was not like I was thinking we would ever be getting married and besides I was *not* his girl. My thinking had not gone that far into the future. Sometimes I don't understand men, but they are who they are, so recognize. They only stayed together married and living together for 62 days, so I won't say what the marriage was based on, and I may never know that part. I don't think anyone living knows that part either. However, he wasn't happy. He told me that much when he saw me during that 62-day event. He acted like sad puppy. I don't think he understood that move himself.

In the Meantime

In the in between time. On another shocking day, my brother was shot and killed in Brooklyn on Halloween night. So, I asked Petie to take the ride with me into the city. This time he had to comfort me. I was in shock and so he drove me to my family. This time was a blur also, because it was shocking, devastating and I was angry. This time I had a funeral to plan and attend. Don't remember when we connected again, but we did.

Petie had been through a lot, more than I can speak of and he had seen a lot in his 38 years of life already. He had hopes and dreams, and I knew I wanted some of his dreams to come true, without interrupting my life. I think he had more of an effect on me than I had on him, or maybe not. Yet one day led to the next and one thing led to another, as he still made me weak in the knees, his voice made my heart flutter like a 16-year-old *silly* schoolgirl. I could not see that good, even with glasses, but I could spot Petie walking on our small-town street a mile away. He had that OG walk. Then every time I heard his voice on the phone, which was usually unexpected, he would catch me off guard and call my job to make a date. When I answered the phone and said hello, there was a pause and he would say "hey J_," and oh my goodness my heart would fall 40 feet. The way he said my name took my breath away, as no one else called me by that name. This was a nice interruption to my usual very busy day at work. Petie probably knew what he was doing now, but I didn't want him to think he was getting to me because he was messing with my mind. I think he tried to act cool and aloof.

Once his voice said the first syllables (we didn't have caller ID back then—LOL), he had my attention, then I had to adjust my brain to hear the rest of the conversation. I would think, "what is this that is happening to me, what am I doing and why am I acting crazy?" Even just to go to Carvel or to the local diner, for a late-night meal, which started to become very regular. He was really smooth and stayed on his best behavior, for the most part, and I liked that. He treated me very special, and I loved that. I was not one of his party friends, because I didn't drink or smoke, and he didn't do that around me for the most part, he would roll a joint to smoke elsewhere. I think he may have just connected with me when he needed a break from those behaviors and that environment. Because he knew my relationship with God, he once told me, "Girl, that's why I deals with you." That still makes me laugh. We seemed to be making up for lost time. On one of our dates, he brought me **his now signature yellow rose**, with a hand printed note that said: *"smell the rose, watch out for the thorns." I probably should have taken heed to that,* and I'm pretty sure I still have that note. He always used words that were well thought out, purposeful and effective. That yellow rose signified our friendship, and I guess he was looking for more than that now we were grown folk, but our friendship was sealed and would be our ground floor.

I had survived a lot of years, and thought I knew how to guard my heart, but he came in and knocked me off my feet, and off my game. I really didn't have much of a game anyway. I was falling back in love, and I couldn't stop myself, and I didn't really want to stop. I didn't know if I should go, because I didn't think this love could or should go anywhere. I was really separated now and had three little children. Yet it was an old familiar feeling, and after so many long talks, long walks and embraces, I felt in a safe place, and I felt my heart could rest with him. It was a battle with my flesh, but it was an everyday battle and because Pete could understand any reservations, as we grew up with the same Word, so he didn't press me much. We had major fun just laughing and talking. He enjoyed my presence because I was on a *natural high* on life, and he would remark about that part. I was that person that didn't like to start new, because that would have been too much work, and this was not something I set out to do, and he didn't seem like a threat, until he was. I was glad he was an old friend. Sometimes my emotions were all over the place. I wasn't sure what to do with them. It was a battle between my flesh, my heart and my spirit. It was a place I thought I left as a teenager, but he had me going in circles. I was grown up and thought I could be responsible and handle myself. I don't even know why, maybe I was just rebounding hard from a failing relationship. My daughters were a constant reminder of that. Petie would tell me he knew that his heart was safe with me. When he looked into my eyes, he could tell I was making a space for him, and he made me smile again, and I did the same for him. Sometimes he was like a giddy schoolboy. He knew that whenever he was hurt or sad, he could come to my shoulder if he needed to cry. He felt free to talk and really felt free to cry real tears with me. I wish I could say they were crocodile tears, but they were not. He had a lot going on deep down inside. It was stuff I didn't see and couldn't imagine, as smart as I thought I was in my thirties. I can remember sending him one red rose in a taxicab (Smith family Taxi) to his job. That move was probably bold and a little forward, but I wanted him to smile and feel my love and sincere care for him. He did, but he was cool about it.

We hung out a lot, when I could, but sort of secretly. That was not comfortable for either one of us. I always tell young people about holding onto their reputation, especially if you are a female, so I had to pay attention to my own. He shared with me a few times that he wanted to live with me on an island. So, I built an **oasis** for him in my heart, but literally, I really couldn't get with that plan, especially with no JCPenney or Macys, that thought was crazy. LOL. I don't think he could have pulled that off anyway. Besides, I had daughters. I knew I had to be an example before them. One of the places Petie wanted to travel was to the New Orleans Mardi gras, but he never did. I don't really think he would have liked it, especially since he didn't like crowds. I think he would have been traumatized.

Decisions Must Be Made

I had a lot of decisions to make, and I didn't want to make the wrong move. After all, I had God, children, and young people at the church to consider. They would all be watching closely. I knew God was always watching. We fell in love again for real, like **when we first began**, but now we were grown up, legal and had to be responsible for our actions. **Our song was "Baby Come to Me."** I got that song from "Luke and Laura" from "All My Children." Silly me. Sometimes I was not sure of his love for me, but I guess I could always tell when he was serious, by the look in his eyes, and as he always said, his heart was safe with me. No games, as we were too old for that, besides the fact, we had both been wounded by love before.

At some point earlier in time, I attempted to talk to my Pastor (WHW-Sr) about our relationship. I was scared because he was like my father and because I didn't want him to be surprised or disappointed in me for being with Petie, even though he knew him from a child. Besides, my Pastor performed my first wedding. Getting married a second time was a far reach. I was also a Youth Leader in my church, and I had to be an example. I think I also wanted Godly instruction from someone I trusted with my spiritual life. I knew my pastor would keep it real and tell me the truth. He knew both of us from children, and he knew our parents. We were close, like family and many times we would spend time after church going over church stuff. That's when I thought I could open up to him, but the words wouldn't come out of my mouth. All of my friends knew him, as we all grew up in church together. I was also at risk of passing the point of no return, so I had to stop and rethink my decisions. I could almost feel a reckless change and I kept trying to be strong. I knew I could not play with fire, and I had to keep my mind right. We were passing the point of holding hands and kissing. I fought my flesh like heck, unfortunately, most men don't feel that same fight. I just wanted truth from an outside source, and I wanted someone else to hear my heart and know my dilemma. I needed someone who could think straight, as I may not have been thinking straight. Our saving grace was that we had never been intimate in our 25-year relationship at that point.

I always believed the Bible, the Pastor, and my wedding vows, which said "until death do us part." Of course, I looked in the Bible for a word to confirm the questions about divorce, which was likely to happen, and I was scared. Clearly, I had to make a choice. I was really getting divorced and felt badly about that part of my life which was falling apart. NOT LOL. That part seemed like a failure, a death, especially when I had received the papers in hand. I didn't know what I was doing any more. Reality hit, it was too real, sad, scary, a no turning back situation, and final. I really didn't want to disappoint God though, and I didn't want to hurt Jesus, because I deeply loved them with all my whole heart, and God had never failed me. He was the only one who was always there for me. I knew God, because I was in relationship with Him. I was strong in the Word, but my flesh was in a battle and getting a little weak. I knew God could get me out of this jam, but I had to be a willing participant. My pastor had been a pastor to both of us during our early lives. I needed help, at least I thought I did.

Most of the time Petie would say how much he cared for me, but that was not the same as saying the word love. I had to patiently wait for that word. I felt it, but I couldn't bring myself to say it first, just in case he was not really feeling the same way. He was a man of many words, and I knew he knew that word. I learned something about him, as he didn't say something he didn't mean. Even if it was a temporary feeling. If that's what he said, that's what he meant. Now when he said it, I said it right back to him.

Petie Popped Another Question

Petie did not ask to marry me in a traditional manner. One afternoon as we pulled up in front of Greenpoint Bank on Sunrise Hwy, was when he popped the question. It was a beautiful day, and not a cloud in the sky. Petie exited the driver's side and came around to open my door. (He was driving my vehicle.) Pete usually was a gentleman, as he opened doors and held doors for me. He said, "Hey BJ, do you want to get married?" I thought he was clowning. We both knew that marriage was the only way we could really be together, yet it was not what I expected Pete to do. We had never talked about him and I getting married. We talked about our feelings for each other but not marriage. I thought he was too cool for me, and so he caught me off guard again. Also, he knew God was important to me, and if I was living that life, I couldn't just do anything I felt like doing. Our friend Charles Haynes was with us. (He was a guy I liked in HS, mainly because he could sing, he was a dark-skinned nice-looking chocolate dude.) What is not memorable was my immediate answer, because his question was a little shocking to me. I may not have answered him that day. I really thought he was joking. Maybe I couldn't speak, but I don't remember what I said right then. I was not prepared for that question, and now I don't remember what we were even talking about in the van on the way to the bank. I'm pretty sure since Charles was with us, we were all just clowning. He probably had to get up a lot of nerve to ask the question and he chose a time when we were not alone. Maybe he felt pretty sure of himself. He knew he was getting to me, and did not think I would shut him down by saying no. I also think he took his time about making this move because he knew making this commitment to me, his current lifestyle would have to be adjusted, and he may not have been really ready for that part. He knew there were principles that I stood on and would not be moved, no matter the temptation. Again, living together would never be an option. I could say a lot, but the rest is history.

So, there were no roses or rings, no bended knee, just the question. It would be later that we shopped for wedding rings. I still couldn't believe it. Once I said yes, we were really well behaved in anticipation of our wedding day. When I realized getting married was on the agenda, I had to fully prepare and deal with bringing another man into the lives of my children, in a much different way. He was already "uncle" to them, now he would be stepdad, which might not really fly with my ex-husband.

Even though I was in my thirties, this was still a very grown-up step for me to make alone, and I didn't have anyone to really consult with. Did God allow this to happen? My response would not surprise God, as He knows the matters of the heart. This may be a test I failed badly. My age said "grown," but my mind said, "big baby," and yeah, I was really a little scared. Words like divorce and second marriage made me anxious. Living together was never a thought, as I was held to a higher God standard, so I could not get away with things other people could. I messed up a few things already, but God was still with me, as He didn't throw me out with the bath water. I certainly let Him down, but His love was still there for me to bounce back.

We acted a little formal with each other, like we were newly dating, or maybe now engaged to be married. It felt really nice, but scary and I didn't want to make an irrevocable mistake, yet I still had time to abandon the whole idea. I didn't want to say that out loud and I smile when I think of the time.

We actually went on a few dinner dates and just stared into each other's eyes. We played that game a lot, mostly when we went out to eat. Pete won most of the time, because the glimmer in his eyes and the twitching of his lips, as he tried to hold back his smile, it would make me smile first. As grown as we both were, we were still kids at heart. When we decided we were really doing this, we finally decided that another Pastor would marry us.

By the way, one of our favorite eating spots no longer exists. When I was in New York for a visit, in 2024. When leaving the airport, I passed our diner; it was still standing. However, during my four-day stay, I saw on the news that the diner had a fire in the kitchen and blew up. That made me sad, however I think I took a picture.

I Got Married Again—An Evening of Happy

We got quietly married one very cold night. We had a wonderful evening, and we did a lot of smiling and laughing. We were very happy, like high school sweethearts, with not a real care in the world. You know, we had our favorite go to meal of Chinese Food, and we acted like we had never been married before and didn't know what we were doing. We were not acting like grown folk, but acted so very silly, and not like we were in our mid-thirties, almost forty.

Together we remained living in Amityville. I continued in church and Pete went on occasion. (I mean Easter, programs, etc.—LOL.) He was struggling with some service-related demons, but I could see him in the future and believed he wanted better, quite frankly, he always said he did. His heart was good, *we both knew that part,* no matter what persona he tried to portray to other friends and family. Some of them (family) liked drama, and Pete knew how to feed it to them. Of course, he would combine some of our personal information along with his own rendition of fake news. Hopefully the next generation of friends and family will catch the truth, however it doesn't really matter, because this was our life. Petie had a distinctive handwriting. So, from his handwritten letters, they will know eventually, if they choose.

A Baby Changes Everything

We tried to get help for some issues, we just didn't always go to good resources for some important things. Petie and I had two beautiful children together, our son, my birthday gift was born on my birthday and another beautiful daughter, a thanksgiving present, born on Thanksgiving Day. We also had a loss of two babies in utero. Together, we had a lot on our plates. Now we had a blended family and a lot of children to raise. Our good times were very good, but our bad times were very bad. When Pete was home, he was all in. We had some ups and downs in our marriage, but we would always eventually kiss and make up, because we had that special something—a spiritual background and bonding, that three strand cord that could not be easily broken, a friendship, and of course, the physical thing.

One of our special songs was by *James Ingram, "Just Once."* Sometimes we couldn't figure out where we were going wrong, but we kept trying to make it right, we both had a strong belief in God. So, when we hit the rough spots and there were a few, and because we understood forgiveness, we could with tenderness and loving care, mend those spots back together. Our friendship was never in trouble. He knew he could wake me up, when he couldn't sleep, and we would just talk and talk, sometimes for hours, *for real*. I loved Mr. Elliott to a fault. Our love took us to a sacred place where only true friends and lovers could go. It would knock me off my feet and he knew that. We needed a supernatural power and Divine intervention. We both agreed about that part. We both wanted a healthy, happy, drama free, easy marriage. It was hard work for both of us and thank God we *always talked*.

Good Morning, Sweetheart—Happy Days—A Good Day

There were so many mornings while Petie was getting ready for work, that he would sing to me, while I lay there catching my last few winks. Petie was still a big kid at heart, so he was pretty playful. (When he played, he liked to be the winner.) Singing energized him after he showered and shaved. I knew we were going to have a good day. One of his favorite songs to sing was by Billy Joel—Love you *Just the Way You Are*. I have found another version by Barry White which I play a lot. But when I want to go back to that memory, I listen to Billy Joel. (I thank God that I found in him a special love and not just a lover.)

Name Calling

Petie started calling me by my initials. That made a lot of our friends follow suit, and the name would stay with me for more than 50 years. It was during tender times he would call me BJ. It was during more tender times that he would call me by my middle name, and he called that name, because it was his to call, and nobody else. When he was upset with me, he would call me by my given first name. When he was really upset, he just didn't come home until late, or maybe not at all. When he was acting up, I would call him by his first name. Thank God most of the time it was just Pete. He would sometimes shave his head bald too, when he was mad with me because he knew I liked his hair. This was way back before men and bald heads was a thing.

I will have to admit that it looked good on him. At times, it was just a very hard journey. I understood about being equally yoked and when you are not, it can become a problem. Sometimes it pulled at the very fabric of our marriage but thank God never at our friendship. Our love reflected rays of light, and it made people smile at us. One good thing about Pete, was that it was always easy for him to apologize, and I would always forgive him, even when it was difficult for me. Some issues were difficult to swallow, but we got through it. I honored my husband because he knew how to repent, to apologize, to say he was sorry when he was wrong or when he did wrong. That spoke volumes to me. He did not always change his behavior completely or do things differently, but I watched how he tried, he was intentional. It never brought him pleasure to hurt me, and the hurt would always show on my face, even if I didn't say a word. That always made the difference to me. I know so many folks claim they have wonderful marriages, but I know mine took some hard work and it was far from perfect. What I can say is that we enjoyed this journey, and I don't think I would have wanted to miss this beautiful love affair for anything.

We both loved Luther's music, and we always listened to his signature music. There is a sentence that is funny that I will only put in my life story, and you will have to read that to find out. I don't think I went to Luther's concerts with Pete, as that would have been awkward and way disrespectful. However, on my 40th birthday after my little party, my friend Darlene and I went to see Luther. We got a chance to chat on the premises with actress Kim Coles and Luther's male family member. Darlene recently told me that they invited us back to the apartment, but she's 80 so I don't think that happened otherwise I would somehow really be married to Luther today. LOL. However, I did get a picture holding Luther's hand for about five seconds in his limo. (He was in the limo, I was not.)

Pete loved family and gave good care to the children, as far as discipline and family stuff. He always talked to them about life and sometimes would corner the big ones, and then they would become his captive audience, but they were respectful and listened. The children will remember that part, and how he made them read and use the dictionary. He always told them not to drink or use drugs and give respect to their elders. One additional thing he would always say to his biological children was "to make mommy smile." He never liked it when we became disjointed. After a season of being angry, he always wanted to fix things, the problem was usually me. I held on to the hurt longer. He was a great conversationalist, a saving grace, but I usually quietly pondered things in my heart. Sometimes I would shut down, and Petie hated that part.

Petie kept most negative lifestyle behaviors outside and away from the kids and me. I was grateful for that part. I recalled once that he had come home drunk and must have fallen while he was in the basement. When I came home, he began calling out to me to come to the basement. Of course, I watched too many crime shows and I didn't know what was really going on. I was really too scared to go and help him. It's funny now, but I kept asking my older children if I should go and see about him, as if I was leaving them with my last will and testament, and I would never return from the bowels of the basement. I had never seen him that drunk and unable to stand. That situation must have lasted for a couple of hours, until I prayed and was brave enough to go help him. I found that he was just too drunk to get up the stairs. I felt silly that I left him there so long.

We didn't fight physically, but we gave each other a few emotional scars. I was always sad about that. I will forever be sorry for not being more understanding, and not being more supportive, as now I understand, the extra mile, the long suffering and patience I needed to give to this marriage, that should have been my part, but I have to eventually let it go.

Every time we separated, and those times were too many, it hurt both of us, because *we were never any good apart.* He usually returned with a tap on my window, promising to make nice, and to change to the best of his ability. He was clear that he couldn't do things perfectly, but he was going to give it a shot. I'm sure he felt his charm could be part of the solution. (He was kind of right about that.) He was afraid to be really vulnerable, because he didn't want to be hurt, as if I would intentionally hurt him. Besides I thought he was too tough to feel hurt. Even though I knew he had a soft side, I didn't believe what I knew for sure.

Again, those were the times we talked for hours, and I mean hours, usually during the midnight hours. Those were the times we took time to heal some wounds. He knew when he was being Ralph and when he was being Petie. That was our very private joke. I loved the sweet P in him, and that's all I wanted him to be. We had great expectations of one another. My husband needed me to be the balance in his life. We failed each other too many times. (However, being separated several times, has now caused me to accumulate long letters and voice mails from my sweetheart, my love.) It's funny how your eyes are opened to all your mistakes, when it's too late to make a difference. I pray someone will take advice and not have to deal with a lot of regret. *My dad used to say, one should never have to say, "I wish I had of . . ."*

Our environment started to get a little rough and the

neighborhood was changing. Crack was on the rise and that made me nervous. I didn't want my children to get caught up in the mix. I knew I couldn't watch all of them at the same time. My husband was already part of the climate. I realize that I could have just left them all in the hand of the God whom I trusted.

I had visited Georgia a couple of times and looking from the outside, it appeared to be bright and shiny, with blue skies, green grass, low crime (so I thought), and wide-open spaces. Everybody seemed to greet you with a friendly smile. So, I decided to move to Georgia in 1996, with all of my eight children. (We were now also raising six of my sister's children—GW.) I don't even know how I got so brave, but I heard God say it was time to GO. This was the second time in my life I left the address of my father. In hindsight, I should have looked deeper at Georgia. I felt I had a responsibility to the children. Even though I left my three oldest children, my new grandson, and my new husband, I felt I had weighed my decision, and I was praying and seeking signs from God. When I believed I had confirmation, I left. My older children all eventually joined us in Georgia. I believed Petie would follow us and I needed him to come, because I missed him terribly. I missed the nice part and the crazy. Whenever he would call us, he would just say how much he missed us and the "noise of the house." When he visited, and after a little persuasion from Christopher, our brother-in-love, he made that final move to Georgia. He needed to leave New York anyway, as it was toxic and a lot for him alone, even though he knew God was with him, which he would say almost every day. My older children were also looking out for him, and he stayed connected to them.

Petie finally moved to Georgia. Family life was good for a while, but we both needed to grow up. We had less family-friends-church support in Georgia. There were no real local diners that were open during midnight hours, where we could steal away. My kids actually hated Georgia because they missed their New York life and their friends, and nothing really to do. Church was not even the same. Life was a little hard. It was some years later when one of my YFC kids told me that her mother (Mother Ruth Walker), said to her once, as she recalled a time from the 60's, "that girl sure loves that boy." Seems like Mother Ruth could tell way back then.

I love you *"Still"* "Sweet P."

Your "bottom lady" Your wife B J, Your Boo.

*Petie wrote in a letter . . . that he is **"listening to Luther in his earphones to the song 'Never let me Go' Luther, B J's other husband."** He said he **"fell in love and a journey began 'Love that boy again'!! I just realized how much I need you. love first realized with you, then there is love of family, love of children, first love for the Creator, then the most significant love is love for my baby, my shorty, my ole Lady, my wife."***

"How could I always choose a joint card for you? Simple . . . being in Love . . . the pure undefined love. the love supreme and I'm only in love with you. So, I looked for words that helped me to describe that Love. It was easy, Focus. Love/ you/BJ! Never stop loving you. I couldn't. We always been

in love from day One! Now no matter when, during all the years, our years, even the angry years, in our most secret place we knew we had love for each other. I knew I was in love and even when we were upset—mad! Now this is what I'm saying, Love is a hell of a thing. I'm always in love with you—angry, happy, screaming, I'm in LOVE That's deep inside—soulful. I'm a husband, I mean a lover. I mean, a friend . . . that is our forte. Our friendship . . . You are my Best Friend. I'm at peace. It is well with my soul. Now I must try to get you to feel my deepest love. God is good . . . All the time."

LAST LETTER . . . "Gave my Creator praise and thanks for mercy, contentment, real inner peace, real outer peace. I am really at peace. I'm on a natural high and I'm finding life to be a grand blessing with the help of the Almighty. God is really good to me!"—Sept. 16, 1998.

One of the favorite songs of his mother was, *"It is well with my soul"* and so some of the last words Pete said and wrote were the same, *"it is well with my soul."* All three of us loved Psalms 91 all very important words.

Epilogue

You reached out to me in Sunday School, when I was 10 years old, and you touched my heart with puppy love. But throughout the years, you kept the music playing and found me again when I was 34 and my heart was hurting.

I was happy to marry my friend and proud and honored because he was a Viet Nam Veteran. He served his country as he was asked to do. I proudly wear his tee shirt that reflect his sentiments. The psychological pressures of the Viet Nam war were certainly overwhelming, as well these left untold invisible emotional scars. You came home as an indirect casualty of war. The scars were partially physical and partially emotional. Those were the scars from Nam that you really never overcame, however you gave it your best shot.

You made it better because we were still the best of friends until we became the best of lovers. From then I wanted to wake up every morning and see your face and feel your heart beating next to me every night. Even those times you caused me heartache and I had to shed some tears, you then found 100 ways to make me smile again, and you succeeded.

You always called me at the right moment, and even though I sometimes expected the calls, or the tap on my window, I was **"STILL"** pleasantly surprised when I heard your mellow voice on the other end of the line. You showed me you loved me by the look in your eyes and the way you held me close. I can really see that look every time I see your picture. But now, when I can't see or touch your face, I still remember your smile.

You gave me precious memories and two beautiful children, one boy and one girl. I loved the way you said the word perfect. Then you added "that God's gifts are always purrfect." We stayed connected for better and worse. We shared a lifetime together, close to half a century and every time I hear your name, my heart "STILL" falls apart. I honored my promise to love you and care for you in sickness and health, and I did that to the best of my ability. That yellow rose remains close to my pillow to make me smile because my heart hurts so badly. I suppose that the music never ends. Your love and friendship will never be replaced. Evergreen. I will never forget your beautiful smile, and I'm glad I didn't miss the opportunity, our second chance to share that love. I could not even imagine doing this life if you had not been a part of it. When you left me, my heart **"Still"** keeps a **"no vacancy"** light on.

Every time I close my eyes, I think about you and I'm **"STILL"** in love, and when we meet in heaven, I expect that we'll fall all over again.

Poem by Maya Angelou

"The sun has come. The mist has gone.
We see in the distance . . . our long way home.
I was always yours to have. You were always mine.
We have loved each other in and out of time."

A Poem for You "A Viet Nam Veteran"

The Essence of You—written Veterans Day 2024

I miss so many things about you
I miss your strong hands that held me,
Your soft heart that kept me close.
The way you moved, the way you kissed
enough to take my breath away.

The way you smiled and made me laugh
The way you talked in a whisper,

through your teeth and pursed lips, so no one
knew you were making a crazy remark.

I miss the way you walked when you
stepped into the hood, you put your cool glide on.
I guess so people would think you were a bad dude.

I miss your brilliance and your words that
made you sound so intelligent.
I miss your laughter and your tears,
because you made me laugh and cry too.

I miss the serious soft look in your eyes,
when you looked at me and
that established our friendship,
it settled our relationship forever.
You talked me through my insecurities,
to remind me of who I am.
I loved the way you researched anything
that you didn't know how to do.
You taught yourself and
You taught me many things too.
I watched you both care and not care.

I miss the cards, you brought or sent me
and the surprise of a single yellow rose,
you would bring me for no particular reason,
and maybe you had one, but just didn't say,
but it would definitely then, be a very good day.

Your letters were long, heartfelt,
thought provoking, warm and humbling.
The outer envelopes made me smile too.
I miss the times we would make love
in the middle of the day, anywhere.

In your last 60 days of life,
You sent me Donnie Hathaway's
"A Song for You," on cassette, Thank you.
Sometimes it was a heavy load,
but I carefully held your heart too.

You said, I was your "best friend,"
Then said, "Girl, I got a thing for you."
Boy, did you know, "I had a thing for you too"?

Thank you for the little things,
and the two special gifts
you gave me, that God delivered.
It was on two very special days,
My birthday and Thanksgiving.
Perfectly, Purr-fect

I miss the cool you and the crazy you too,
I MISS YOU, my Brave Air Force Man,
I MISS YOU, my Sweet Music Man,
I MISS YOU, my Sweet Boo.
*And **"STILL"** I cry, I really cry,*
*And **"STILL"** I smile too. **BJE***

8

Jeanette and Keith's Love Story

My Story—A Divine Appointment

The collision course that led to my husband (Keith) and I meeting, flowed through the channel of people that knew both of us. They were members of a home-based bible study. I had known them for a few years prior to the start of that home-based bible study. These people kept bragging with plenty excitement on how well Keith taught. They kept saying to me you just have to come hear him teach. Finally, I made my way to the bible study. I must say that the bible study was very interesting. Pastor Keith was very personable and engaging with our group.

After attending several meetings, Pastor Keith shared something very personal of himself. He talked about his family and more specifically, his younger children. He stated that at that time he was living separate from them and wanted to be a part of the lives of his children before they were grown. He had been afforded that opportunity of doing so, in the lives of his three older girls. He wanted to experience the same kind of relationship with his younger children.

Many of the group members stated they would love to assist him in any way they could, if he brought them from New Orleans to Georgia. I stated also that if he got his children, I would be willing to help and support him in that effort. I was very impressed that a father would step up to personally care for his children.

Test Time

Test time arrived! The children were out of school and only the two youngest ones were able to come and visit with him for a short period. Pastor Keith observed firsthand my keeping the promise of helping him with them. It was during a reception that was held in regard to an event with the bible study group. He brought the children to the event that night. Pastor Keith was so impressed with the ease of how I attended to them during the reception that upon departing the event, from that night on, he began to declare to me, that "you're going to be my wife." I of course laughed and shrugged him off. Marriage was the furthest thing from my mind during that phase of my life. To add to that fact, marrying a minister was definitely not my desire. A man of God absolutely, but not a minister. "No way José," was my genuine feeling.

Keeping My Word

When the time came, Pastor Keith got his children, and I kept my word. When he saw that I was really going to help him, he was amazed and happy. This may have been a lot for him alone, so I knew I had to step up to the challenge. With the help of God, I assisted him, unfortunately I happened to be the only one that did what I promised to do. I was single so this challenge pretty much did not interfere with my life. However, I did not have a "normal single life." My single life was pretty busy, as I found myself always being pulled in so many directions to assist other people. Then one day Pastor Keith said to me, "you're going to be my wife." I just laughed and thought nothing much about it. Then almost every time he saw me, he would say the same thing.

I believe Pastor Keith got my message, and we continued to talk. I also had gotten a part time job, which he was unhappy about, as he felt it would take time away from him and the children. I also had to tell him, that he never asked me to be his wife, he just said I was going to be his wife. Now the ball was in his court. I also had to tell him, that because he had been married before, that he needed to make sure he made time to heal from that relationship, before moving on to another one. He was a little upset about my revelations concerning this relationship. So, he didn't call me for a few days.

I told him that my relationship as a woman of God and a single woman, was serious. Reminding him that he had already been married with children, and that was something I had not yet considered. His next response was, "what are you afraid of?" I had to let him know that I was a real woman of God, and I was completely sold out to the Lord. I had no time for games.

He finally decided to pop the question in 2000. My answer

was a firm yes with conditions. The condition was that if I said yes, we would have to wait until 2002. At first, he said that would be fine. So, we went to marriage counseling for people who wanted to get married. We completed the counseling and for the most part it went smoothly. I was now in my late thirties, and he was in his early forties.

We Got Engaged

So, one night he asked me "what was I afraid of" as it relates to marriage. I shared my thoughts and explained to him leaving a single life to getting married to a man with children. Not only that part but also marrying a minister. He began to understand my hesitation. In addition to that, I said to him, "by the way, you never asked me to marry you." Then he finally decided to pop the question in 2000. So, at that point, I knew he came to his senses, and he asked, "will you marry me?"

My answer a firm "yes" but conditional ball back in my court. The condition was that if I said yes, we would have to wait until 2002. At first, he said that would be fine. He agreed and said that's just what the Lord had spoken to him. So, we went to marriage counseling for people who wanted to get married. We completed the counseling and for the most part it went smoothly. I was now in my late thirties, and he was in his early forties. However, people began to get in his ear, asking him what was holding up the wedding. So, he began to pressure me. I reaffirmed the conditions, and he wanted to get married right then.

The Breakup

I moved out and he moved in. Pastor Keith worked very hard for his children, and I was happy to help. He got an apartment for his children to reside, and after talking it over with the children's mother, I would also become a part of their lives. I stayed in the apartment with the children, as I had prepared it for them before they actually got there. Occasionally, he would buy a gift for me as a gesture of his appreciation. We talked a lot on the phone, and I knew it was time to make things very clear and up front with Pastor Keith. He was also a man of God that kept things 100 with people. He said just what he meant. Our conversations were mainly about the ministry and then we would sometimes discuss his children. Our relationship and friendship grew a little deeper.

He still maintained that I was going to be his wife. However, when he began to put the pressure on concerning moving up the time for marriage, I wanted to stick to God's plan. So, I moved out and he moved in with his children. He was a little upset with me, and we didn't speak for a brief while.

Finally He Reached Out—We Faced Another Problem

I saw his genuine care and concern for me, he really showed his interest in me, I knew now I had feelings for him. I knew how sincere he was when he made a great sacrifice as it related to his job. I had told him that my doctor wanted me to have a biopsy, but I would need someone to be my driver. He said that even though his position as manager required him to be present on that same day, he made the decision to accompany me to my appointment. He trusted God to handle his job. This spoke volumes to me as it showed me that he placed my situation as a priority when I needed him, in order to drive me from my doctor's appointment. This was shortly after we became engaged. Earlier I had let him know that my doctors were concerned and wanted me to have this biopsy. He prayed for me and agreed to be my driver. He trusted God to handle his absence from his job. Days later he discovered that this was the first time his restaurant had received one of their highest scores. Now I was impressed. He showed me that I was a priority. We continued to talk many days after this appointment. I felt now our relationship had gone to a new level, so the wedding was back on again.

It was good that we kept our lines of communication open and straight forward. We always had deep conversations, and the Lord was with us. We needed to get the blood test for our license first. Once we did that, now we were pretty much ready to walk down that aisle as husband and wife.

The Blood Test Found New Problems

Once we were back on track to be married, we needed to get our blood tested. We went to take care of that part. A few days after the test, my phone rang. It was Pastor Keith's doctor's office. They had been trying to reach him, but he hadn't returned their call. So, I give him the message. When he got in touch with his doctor, they had him come in and they let him know that he was facing some health issues that were cause for concern. At that visit, he was diagnosed with diabetes and hypertension. His numbers were alarmingly high, so much so that he could have slipped into a coma. So then made sure that he got immediate attention for the medical concerns. We continued with our counseling and our last counseling session was the night before we were to be wed. We had so much going on and a lot to do for our big day. We were busy. We also had to attend a dinner reception that folks were throwing for us.

Wedding Day We Still Got Married in 2002

As God would have it, we still made it to our 2002 wedding date. The day was very chaotic, but it turned out fabulous. Even with all of the challenges we went through, we were in love and very happy. Life was a true adventure; it was challenging but God was holding to His promise of guiding us through our blended family, with more to come on our love journey. But now the rest is history.

9

Barbara and James's Love Story

It was a hot summer day in Springfield, Mass., in 1971. I had just graduated from college in Hamden, Connecticut. and was working in my first job at Springfield Hospital, Blood Bank Lab. I was just beginning my career as a Clinical Laboratory Medical Technologist. This was my first job after graduating from college. I was renting a one-bedroom apartment within walking distance to the hospital where I was working.

As a "hobby" or pastime, I indulged in photographic and modified run-way modeling. It was all for fun, and it was certainly not my "day job." Prior to my part time modeling in Springfield, Massachusetts, I had finished a course in modeling at a local modeling school in Hartford, Connecticut. It was while I was finishing my senior year in Hartford when I met Ted Beaudin, who owned his own Photography business and worked with the modeling school's director, Joyce. After moving to Mass. from Conn. Ted & I kept in contact. On one hot, humid summer day, Ted called me and invited me to participate in an amateur photographers' weekend convention as a model. This event was going to be held at UMass. campus at Amherst, Massachusetts. All the models would need to do was stroll around the beautifully landscaped campus grounds making ourselves available to be photographed by some ham photographers. I had just come out of a romantic relationship and thought doing something like this on a "lazy and warm" summer weekend, would be mentally and emotionally good for me. So, I accepted the invite and Ted and I drove up to UMass. to attend the convention.

It was either on that Saturday or Sunday, while strolling about the campus, posing for photographers, he asked to photograph me, that I met a Professor from Dartmouth College School of Medicine. Dr. Grey politely asked if he could photograph me and I again I accepted.

While posing and being photographed, he and I conversed about our backgrounds, sharing what we did for a living. He told me he was a professor of microbiology at Dartmouth Medical School, in Hanover NH. I in turn told him I was a new Clinical Laboratory Medical Technologist working in a Blood Bank at Springfield Hospital, Mass., and that I had just graduated from college, in June of 1970. The supposed agreement was that, in lieu of payment, these photographers were supposed to share copies of the prints and or projector slides, taken of the models. After returning back to Springfield and work, several weeks later, I received a manilla envelope in the mail, from Dr. Grey. The envelope contained a few slides and prints (photos) that Dr. Gray had taken of me that convention weekend. Along with this material was a handwritten note, stating that a certain medical student had seen some of my photos on display across from Dr, Grey's office. This medical student, Jim, questioned his professor about how he met me. He then asked Dr. Grey for my phone number, as he wanted to contact me. Of course, Dr. Grey was very respectful of my privacy, so in his note to me, he asked my permission to give my phone number to this inquisitively interested medical student. Since, I was no longer in a romantic relationship, and had more "time on my hands," I replied to Dr. Grey, giving my permission to him to share my contact information with this medical student.

It was about two or three weeks later that I received the anticipated call from James. His baritone voice, with a "hint" of Black Southern dialect, sounded interesting to me. From the sound of his voice, I remember, picturing him as being an older man, who perhaps had taken a "gap" year off from under-grad school, and decided to pursue medical school later.

In my mind, I pictured him to be much older than I with perhaps, some early signs of balding and greying, at the tem-ples. All of this illustration was in my mind, based just on the sound of his voice. Along with the interestingly engaging voice he had a "way with words," and that kept me very interested in what he was discussing with me. I didn't want the conversa-tion to end. From the first time we spoke to each other, it was almost surreal, indeed.

During that first phone conversation, James shared with me, that he was a director that summer, of a "Bridge Program" on the Dartmouth College campus. The purpose for that

Program was to assist high school students endeavoring to enter the field of Medicine and the Allied Health Field. Dartmouth College School of Medicine was anxious to recruit "minority" students, to apply to the Ivy League school. James had been told by Dr. Grey, that I was a Clinical Laboratory Medical Technologist, working in the Allied Health Field. With that being said James cleverly invited me to come up to the College to speak informally to these students about my field of work. I accepted the invitation assuming that I would be one of several other speakers invited to attend.

The day I drove up to the College, it was rather hot and mildly humid. I had just returned home from attending a wedding in Ossining, NY, of a good college friend. I quickly changed into a sheath summer dress and put my "afro" wig on and styling it quickly. I quickly got on the road on my way to meet, in person, this "Doctor-in-the-Rough," named James, Jr. in order to arrive at the time Jim & I had agreed upon.

Well, the drive up to Dartmouth College, in Hanover, NH, from Springfield, Mass., on that warm, sunny summer day was quite pleasant. Upon my arriving at the campus gate at Dartmouth Medical School, Jim was contacted at his dormitory. So, there I sat in my car waiting for Jim to arrive to meet me. Of course, the mental picture I created in my mind, based on hearing his voice, dominated my thoughts as I anxiously awaited his arrival. The wait wasn't long, before I noticed a rather large, dark colored auto pull up just beyond the gate entrance to pause, parallel to my parked car. As I gazed at the vehicle, anxiously looking to see Jim's face. I saw this young-looking man, with the most gorgeous smile and beautiful teeth, "grinning from ear-to-ear," as he drove up to my car. His appearance did not fit the prefabricated "picture" of him that I had created in my mind, not in any "way, shape or form." His appearance didn't fit the almost baritone voice with a strong Black Southern dialect that I heard over the phone. So, as I tried to constrain myself, I smiled a "glad to see/meet you" type of smile back at him.

He didn't get out of the car he was driving but beaconed me to follow him. So, I did, to the dormitory in which he resided. In getting out of our respective cars, he approached me, as I was getting out of my car. I was somewhat surprised that he wasn't as tall or as old, as I had imagined he'd be. But he was handsome, sporting that "million dollar" smile. Much later, in our relationship he expressed to me how he was surprised that I was as "tall" as I was, then. Actually, I thought he was kind of short for a man. I was 5'8" at that time. So, in general, some would assume that was tall for a woman. I was also a "skinny girl." That's the second reason I did well in my "modeling hobby."

As we walked up to each other and probably shook hands, formally greeting each other, Jim told me we would be going to one of his professor's homes, a short distance away, in the Vermont hills, for the informal gathering. He then took me to his room to rest up a bit, from the drive, to talk, getting more acquainted. Jim was the "perfect gentleman" After about an hour, we drove, in my car, a few miles away to Dr.

& Mrs. Margolis's home. How excited I was to see Dr. Clarke Gray, the "photographer" who photographed me at the UMass. at Amherst, Mass. "Ham" Photographers' Convention. He would later be known, by his family, as "Cupid," especially concerning how Jim and I met. It was, as mentioned earlier, through my photos, displayed in a display case, right outside of Dr. Gray's office. Jim, in passing, saw my photos and eventually stopped to ask Dr. Gray about me.

At that gathering Clarke had more photos to give me that he developed in his "dark room" next to his office. I was not surprised to learn from Jim, a little later, that he'd already seen the photos, that Clarke was turning over to me.

As Jim and I entered Margolis's home, I was quickly introduced to both he and his wife, Ann. The house smelled of something delicious being cooked, by Mrs. Margolis. There were about five students, participants in that summer's "Bridge Program" sitting on the carpeted living room floor. Jim, Clarke and I sat on the back deck of the house talking about the photographs and having a general conversation. I turned around looking for the "other speakers," whom Jim told me would be attending. Well Jim, as I would learn later, had a very good "way with words." When I asked him "Where are the other speakers?" He replied, coyly, "We didn't want to steal your fire." So, there I was, the fairly new college graduate, working in my first job, since graduating, as a Clinical Lab. Technologist, and now learning that I was to be the sole speaker, at that gathering. Well, I was grateful that the gathering was very informal.

By the way, the chili dinner was very good, and helped make the afternoon even more delightful. There was definitely, "no turning back" now. My curiosity in what was beginning to happen, started to peak.

10

Ann and Albert's Love Story

I met my husband, the Love of my life in 1982. I will never forget that time of my life. My friend was dating this guy who I'll call Joe. I used to see Joe every so often when he was dating my friend Sally. I never spoke much, and I was very quiet. One day Sally said that Joe has a friend who he wanted me to meet. He said that he believes that we would hit it off because he's quiet and we would get along quite well together.

The meeting between Albert and I was to take place by him taking me to the Prom. Well that never happened. Several more times we were supposed to meet, and it didn't happen. Of course, I threatened my friend jokingly not to introduce me to someone who is not compatible to me, and yes, I was saved. I was 17 years old at the time. Any way it seemed as if we would never meet, and I was no longer anxious about meeting him. LOL. However, my friends were more anxious. Finally, in order for us to meet, we would speak for the first time on the phone. He called me and boy did I feel silly, and I said so and he agreed too. LOL. We hung up so quick and I said, that was so dumb, I don't even know who I'm speaking to. So then, from that moment, I totally erased it from my mind.

About two weeks later, while I was at my house, here comes my friend Sally. It was Easter Sunday 1982. She said Joe and Albert were on their way right now to my house. I said what?? Anyway, he showed up and we talked a little here and there because Joe and Sally were right there with us. When he was leaving, he shook my hand and said he would call me the next day, and he did. Now we have called each other without fail for the last 41 amazing years. We have not missed a day.

We dated for two years and then got married in 1984. Thirty-nine years, 5 children and 14 grandchildren later, we know that God has blessed us with a beautiful family and we're still holding strong. How was it possible? I'll tell anybody, God had to be the center of our relationship for it to have worked. There were ups and downs and a few rough spots that happened. It's only natural. When you have two people from two different cultures, backgrounds and heritage coming together, joining as one, there are going to be life situations, but prayer helped to bring us through. I was saved and of course sometimes God takes the backseat and the husband the drivers' seat, but I realized at the age of 24, I needed God to be in the driver's seat.

So, I started digging in more so I could understand who this God really was. I began praying for my husband to get saved, I believe it was 21 years later that he gave his life to the Lord. What this meant to me, and I hope others will get the message, that you should never give up. Prayer really will change things. Do we still date? Yes, we do, because that's important to do so. That's my soulmate for life and we take care of each other. When you both pray together, things still may not be as perfect as you would like, but you weather the storms in your life together and get through it.

Albert and I have been married 39 years. This year in 2024 Lord willing, we celebrated forty years of marriage, and no, everything was not perfect, but we worked at our marriage and now we're growing old together. God has been faithful to us.

The day I met my husband was one of the best days of my life. Yes, we are still in love! Again, it took years of learning about each other and understanding one another and learning to not fuss over simple things. Also, one thing I strongly believe in is keeping the lines of communication open at all times. Even when we were upset with each other we talked things out, even if we went to bed in the wee hours of the morning, it didn't matter.

Married couples have to understand that tough times will come, but it takes a tough couple to withstand the pressure and the test of time. I was 21 years old when I got married. LOL. I was a baby and I'm 60 years old now. Many times, when people get married at a young age, they don't survive the marriage, but we had the secret, the third strand, and we did not have an escape plan. I've learned a lot and praise God; Albert and I could not have done it without the Lord!

11

Deloise and Alfred's Love Story

Finding love at age 59, well I know, it may not seem surprising for some, but for me, it was a welcomed **SURPRISE BLESSING**. My love story is brief, nonetheless, it's my story. As a little girl, from humble beginnings, my mother was the mother of seven (7) and a widow at age 32. I was five years old when my dad was killed. I really didn't know what a "love" relationship looked like.

My two older sisters had their first child(ren) at an early age. I was only 14-year-old at the time. I didn't know anything about the "Birds and the Bees," as the senior folks would say, and it certainly wasn't talked about in our household. Upon graduating, I remained very shy, quiet, and kept to myself. Up to that point in my life, I had never had a boyfriend and certainly had never been kissed. After I graduated, I thought it was time for me to step outside my shell.

I got my first job with Levi Strauss & Co. I moved and lived with my cousin in what we called "the old house." My uncle helped me purchase my first car. It was a two-door 1977 Grand Trino Spots blue hardtop with a white bottom. I was so proud of myself. I was enjoying learning about me or what I thought was learning "me."

About two or three years after graduating, my cousin introduced me to a young man who was her brother-in-law and wow, he was sooo handsome. We began dating and I really liked him. We dated until he asked me to marry him. I said "yes."

Our marriage date was February 6, 1981. I was still very naïve about relationships, but we continued to get to know each other better and better. We would talk about so many things, family, our growing up experiences, visiting other states, friends, and what we wanted in life. We both had decent jobs. We talked about how he wanted to join the military and the opportunities it would allow us. Well, that came to pass, and we came to an agreement. He joined the military and thereafter we relocated to another state. He was deployed out of the country shortly after our relocation.

Stay with me now . . . There I was a newlywed, in another state with no family and knowing no one. But with God's grace, He was with me growing me as a newlywed. I loved my husband and missed him so much. We were always writing and making phone calls as much as possible. When the time came for his tour-of-duty to end, we both were excited to be reunited.

Spoiler Alert: Things were different, he was not the calm, low-key loving man I came to know and married. Years later we divorced. Yes, we remained friends. He shared with me years after our divorce that the things he saw (the shootings, bombing, etc.), it caused him trauma and he didn't know how to tell me or how to handle it. We are still family to this day. I learned what the emotions of being in love felt like and I wanted that in my life.

I Wanted to love again. Fast forward, as a single person again, I relocated solo to another state. As I learned my way around my new location, and I was enjoying my singlehood. However, years later, my *"emotions"* were heightened, and I wanted love in my life again, I wanted to be in a loving relationship.

A co-worker told me about on-line dating to meet Godly mature men who were stable and ready for marriage. "Bingo," she showed me how it worked, and I was set and ready for the challenge.

Oh Lord, I didn't know I had to go through so much. I had to go through what we would say in the country "a weeding out." What I can say is that I met some nice guys from that experience, of which, some became like brothers to me.

At one point I told the Lord, I don't care if I kick, squabble, fall out on the floor and have a tantrum, if they were not from Him, remove them and don't let them come near me.

God is funny and faithful.
He cares about us more than we can imagine.

I really enjoyed early morning walking. So, one morning, my friend and I were walking, and she said, "Lady D" what is the Lord saying?" And immediately what dropped in my spirit was **"If they can't see ME (God), they can't see you."**

Wow. . . . In that moment Abba showed me that He cares about me more that I could think or imagine. God was faithful. At that time, I put the on-line dating on ice, and my Heavenly Father kept my emotions in check.

One day my emotions were acting up and I cried out "Lord," how long. I was desiring to be in a Godly, loving relationship and ready for marriage. I got a prompting that it was okay to use on-line dating (it wasn't a sin). Thank God for knowing us better than we know ourselves. He, Father God knew my relationship with Him was not to be tampered with. So there, I decided to give "on-line dating" one last chance. At the time I did on-line dating, it had already been launched for numerous years.

He Said/She Said

I was **very specific** in my on-line profile about the kind of man I desired. Well low and behold, I got numerous replies, but it was something about this one person who reached out to me that got my attention. Mind you, two things about his profile that were **"red flags"** as we call it. He only had one picture, and his status was "legally separated." I thought to myself, "are you kidding me—why are you on here with this mess?" Nonetheless, I replied to him. And the inquisitive, fact-finding person that I am, I needed answers. I replied and asked, "what does legally separated mean?" He later told me that he said to himself "who does she think she is, asking me that?."

And he almost swiped left. But he kept coming back to my profile. He said, "she deserves an answer; she knows what she wants and she's not a game player." We engaged in chatting conversations until we decided we wanted to meet. We decided to meet at a local restaurant. When he got out of his truck, and I knew he was really checking me out, but I had sized him up from head to toe in about ten seconds. Yep, my kind of man.

From our initial meeting we decided we wanted to keep seeing each other. During our courtship, we did so many clean fun things. We dated for about two years and really got to know each other. Then at Thanksgiving dinner with family and friends, he surprisingly asked me to marry him. On October 20, 2018, I married the love of my life at age 59, and the rest is history.

12

Joanne and Victor's Love Story

These are the things that grew me into a constant love for Victor throughout the years—through thick and thin and through ups and downs. He was 26 and I was 18 when our relationship was taken to another level. We were next door neighbors. I didn't realize that he was my Boaz until much later. I loved his character, mind, and body. His big strong hands, muscular and nicely formed arms and legs. I knew him, but I didn't take notice of him as a man that I could be interested in as he was the older brother of my neighbors. However, the day that he began to slowly steal my heart was through his kindness to me "at the fence." I say at the fence because, looking back, that is where we would meet and talk about general things—like—he was not going to stay in America for he was just passing through on his way to England and circled back to Jamaica. He would share with me about his female relationships including the details of those relationships. We talked a lot about our life experiences, mainly his life experiences, as they were more fun.

He was like a story book teller. He had a way of drawing me into his life by creating an illuminating picture or an action or drama movie that I could stand on the side and watch the entire thing unfold. They were all so active and illuminating. I admired the way his love and devotion to his family, barring nothing, to come between them even though his parents would get on him for something he did. He never exposed them in a negative light. I saw him as a protector and a honorable man. There were 2 things that I was looking for and that is a man that provides security, and a man that was family oriented. I loved how he treated his mother, father, sisters, brother, aunts and even his older cousins—all with respect and a deep love. He would do anything for them. I saw that as something that would be transferred to a generation.

God had placed in my heart early in life what to look for in a man that you want to spend the rest of your life with, but I didn't know that it was him as yet. I admired his work ethics and his focus when he was working. I admired how he worked through and came up with solutions without fear of his decision. I admired relationship with his dad, and how they did things together. I saw the power of family. I saw how he treated them, and I knew that he would make a great husband, but I didn't think it would be with me. I was just intrigued by him as a guy, but I didn't know that this was a developing story that would be for me and that it would last 43 years.

In my early friendship forming time with Victor, I enjoyed being with him. He had lots of jokes to share. He was the type of person that would tell his jokes and laugh out loud at them every time and this never changed. It didn't matter whether you got the joke or not, it was on you. That is what I liked about him. I said this man had no shame, because some of his jokes were so bad, but he never stopped telling them. He did not blush to tell the same story over and over and laugh again and again. He never looked for approval of himself and his thoughts. If he did, it was covered up with his laughter and this went on through our entire relationship of 43 years.

I became so comfortable listening to this 25-year-old sharing with me his stories and his life seemed so exciting and dull-less life—a man in charge of himself and I liked that. I enjoyed this friendship and actually never felt that I was going beyond that. Victor had a car, and he was always willing to take my friends and I anywhere we asked. I always knew that I had a ride home from any parties that I attended. I felt protected, loved, cared for when I was with him, but I didn't get it. Maybe I didn't understand much at the time but as time went by, I should have gotten it, right? Because he would do whatever I asked him to do, but I didn't so he waited.

Looking back, I believed that even though I knew what to look for in a man, maybe my looking glass was a little smeared by past teen relationships and my peers that had spoken into my ears, and some things I had seen.

Victor was a unique man indeed. He strongly believed in doing what was right and what was fair. He was always willing to help a neighbor, a friend, a stranger. This character never changed. These were the things that kindled my heart and kept it burning with love. This was not just his love for me, but it was also his love for others. His love was constant and not based on what I did or did not do. He was like a Boaz. Now this may sound strange to some, but it was not things that he gave me or said to me that drew me to him. For example, he would say, "I love how your eyes glimmer in the candlelight," or "how perfect that dress looks on you"—*even though he did*. So, my relationship didn't start with a wink, a hug or flowers on valentine's day or a "hey beautiful girl, I love the way you carry yourself." No, it was my observation of a manly man. Also let me interject with this, he was not perfect, by no means, he was perfect in my view. LOL. If he had flaws, I didn't know it or see them. LOL. Remember, I said from the time we were friends to dating and going steady, that was my view. I saw the flaws later.

One evening Victor pulled up to my driveway and asked me if I wanted to go to the movies, so I said, "yes." At that time, I still considered us just good friends, a friend that was fun and a friend that I admired. So, we started going to the movies on Thursday nights in my senior year. In hindsight though, I think that he was admiring me more than I thought, but he hid it well and he did nice things for me without calling attention to it.

We enjoyed each other's company on Thursday nights and looked forward to it. After the movies, we would go to White Castle, and he would have coffee and I would have two fish burgers with cheese. He would just watch me eat but I was a slow eater, so sometimes, he would help me by finishing off my sandwich, even though he never ate after dinner or snacked between meals. I believe that he was showing me that he didn't mind eating after me. He would do that and look at me with a love look, if you know what I mean. Oh, I forgot to mention, from our movie dates, slowly we began to kiss. When he first asked me for a kiss, after he dropped me home one night, I gave him my cheek, but he refused. After our first kiss, oh yes, there was a heart connection!! My heart began to connect to his, now in a different way. It was like an invisible cord from his heart to mine. As his was ready and waiting, it took a minute, then I just opened up my heart for his to get into mine. Again, looking back, I believed that it started with my observation of him and of my admiration of my friend, Victor.

I just didn't see it or get it—okay I was a little blind sighted. I believed that's why he prides himself on his nick name "Slick Vic." He observed and he waited, while working on finding a gentle way to my heart. He liked me but he was waiting for me to get it, and he didn't want to chase me away. He told me that much later when he asked me to marry him.

After I graduated from High School, we continued to go out. We had a secret between us that was budding. It was our longing for each other's company that was an underground "knitting in secret"—it was unexplainable and not visible to friends and family, because we didn't announce it. We just "were." It was our secret love affair, but after a while it broke through the ground up into the open earth, visible for others to see and family and friends could see that "hey, there's something going on between these two." We enjoyed each other's company and to verbalize it or announce—you just had to observe the connection as we weren't falling all over each other in the company of others, and we weren't whispering sweet nothings into each other's ears, in company of others, but behind closed doors it was different!! There was something definitely in the formation of the love between us from what I called my budding experience to what kept us for 43 years. It was his character, silent, observing, strong, kind, working on a plan man, and just loving to the core. Oh, how could I forget to mention something women love and that's "romance." He was the most romantic man, well in my eyes, the things that he would do for me to make my heart smile, were beyond that which includes physical and emotional wows.

13

Janiese and Cody's Love Story

I met Cody 6 years ago in 2019 at a party. I was 19 years old and very into partying at the time as I joined the Navy after a failed college attempt. I was practically an adult in my eyes. He says he came to use the bathroom, and I did not lock the door, but he tried to leave. He says I locked him in there and sat on the corner and talked to him. At the time he was a cowboy, with boots and his pants tucked into his pants but even then, he was a gentleman. We remained friends for years as we worked at the same place and always saw each other. It wasn't until 2023 that I noticed him as a love interest in my life. I was nervous about dating a white man since I had never dated outside of my race before. I remember our first date like it was yesterday. We went to Total Wine and Chillis and saw a movie. After that, I dragged him into Target and we bought pointless things, but I felt comfortable with him. Our marriage story isn't that exciting though. Before we got married, we discussed it, and Cody talked to my mother to see if he could marry me. We got married a few months later. I wasn't scared, I was nervous because marriage is a massive step in anyone's life. I didn't have the appropriate examples of what a proper marriage should be.

So far, my life with Cody has been amazing. I fell in love with him because of his attentiveness. How much he cares about my happiness. We have been away from each other for over 6 months due to both being military, but I can say that I wouldn't trade him for anything in the world. He is the sweetest man and supportive of me in all that I do. I protect him because he is my best friend. If I had to tell my younger self anything it would be to never doubt yourself! Never give up on yourself and cherish everything that comes and comes in your life good or bad. Also, I love you so much. I learned that the most meaningful love is between themselves and God. After that, nothing can take your joy away.

14

Judith and Wilson's Love Story

Wilson and I met on purpose! For purpose! I began working at Wolmer's Boys school as a mathematics teacher in 1996 where I met Wilson for the first time. He was starting as the guidance counselor for the school, and we were in the same new teachers' seminars.

At the end of the day, my dad came to the school to pick me up and was about to take me home, when I saw Wilson. He appeared to have a disability, as he seemed to have difficulty walking. I offered to take him to a place where he could take the bus home, so my soft heart thought that I should help him. I found out he was a Christian, and besides that, he was a missionary who came to Jamaica to spread the gospel. I was captured by his stories about New Zealand, Fiji and Tonga. He had completed his masters in Missiology.

In college I was so intent on becoming a missionary myself, but the Lord said to me that i should complete my degree and to be a giver to missions as I worked. So, this was my first indication of God's purpose being unfolded in my life.

We decided to start the Christian club in the school. We called it Inter-Schools Christian Fellowship (ISCF), as our own way of spreading the gospel among the young people that we served.

This was the beginning of our friendship and eventually our work together. We started hanging out consistently. He played the guitar, so I introduced him to my Christian friends who played in a band. We would come together each evening singing and worshiping. He eventually started coming to the same church as myself, which was called Mona Fellowship at the time. Until this point, we were just friends.

I enjoyed talking with him and we interacted a lot. One day he asked me to go to a concert using the story that he bought two tickets, the second was supposed to be for his friend, but his friend could no longer go. So, he said he was wondering if i would like to go to the concert with him. When I said yes to his invitation, but I wanted him to be clear, that this was not going to be a date. So, I just took the ticket and went on my own with my sisters.

The concert turned out to be only three minutes from my house, so I walked to the event. That night however, I had this feeling, and I became aware of a spiritual connection with him. It seemed that I could sense his presence before I could even see him. It was so surreal. I was shocked.

Even though I didn't consider this to be a date, that he secretly wanted, we ended up spending the whole evening together anyway. So technically this was our first date. I didn't know I was falling for him, because I was so young and naive,

I just thought I loved hanging out with him and enjoying his company. I found him to be so different from the men I met from home. He was Nigerian, well-traveled and well exposed to the world. I was very impressed with his knowledge of the world, and I loved to listen to all of the stories of his travels.

15

Lisa and Michael's Love Story

In the heart of Atlanta, our paths finally converged after three decades apart. Michael, once the mesmerizing pop locker, had gracefully transitioned into the world of film, while I, a retired hairstylist and emergency room tech, found purpose in coaching women on the mends.

The reunion sparked memories of those high school days, where Michael's dance moves made my heart skip a beat. Now, with life's tapestry woven through marriages, children, and careers, our connection rekindled.

Our love story, however, took a surprising twist, and it began with a divine nudge. We share a love for travel, dance, and singing, each adventure a spicy note in the melody of our romance. But beyond the dance floor, our love is an intoxicating cocktail—a heart-sinking arrow of passion and laughter, a sexy-hard-time symphony that plays between us. Back when we were younger, we danced and laughed, our hearts were free and unburdened by the weight of responsibilities. Those were the days when the pop lock dance was our language, and I, a freshman, would stand in awe as Michael, a senior, would tear it up on the dance floor. Little did I know that years later, destiny would bring us back together in a different dance, the dance of love. We think together, pray together, and love God together. Michael, with his big, knowing eyes, understands the language of my body's desires. He's the remedy to my hurts, the bearer of creams that soothe my soul. God sent him to me; he is my heart, my real "okay."

It all began when, seated in that chair, when I asked God to send me my husband. He did exactly that, whispering in my ear to call Michael. I hesitated, thinking, "but that's not my husband." Yet, destiny had a different plan. Swallowing my doubts, I called him, craving a hug. We met at Pappadeaux's parking lot, a rendezvous that became a turning point. As Michael's arms wrapped around me, a small kiss on my lips ignited a wind of emotions—an uncharted territory of love that felt meant to be. It was a man-please-don't-let-me-go kind of feeling, like God had orchestrated our reunion. Two months later, we moved in together; two months after that, we said our vows.

Eleven years of marriage have passed, but every kiss still sparks that same unshakable feeling. Our love story, a blend of sexy serendipity, laughter, and the sweet symphony of two souls rediscovering each other again and again. Our journey continued to unfold, marked by shared dreams and a growing passion for each other. Our travels became a canvas for new adventures, each destination a backdrop for the next chapter in our love story. Whether dancing under foreign stars or singing our hearts out in a karaoke bar, we embraced the joy of doing things together like never before. As Michael pursued his filmmaking endeavors, I reveled in coaching women, finding fulfillment in helping heal broken hearts. Our love became a guiding force, a beacon that illuminated the path we walked together. Our days were woven with laughter, inside jokes, and those lingering kisses that never lost their magic. And so, our love story continued, an ever-evolving saga of passion, growth, and an unwavering connection.

Through the highs and lows, our love remained the anchor, the sweet melody that played in our hearts, making every moment together feel like a scene from a perfectly written script.

16

Stephanie and Anthony's Love Story

Meet Stephanie and Anthony, and trace the Hand of God in their lives, as they discover the faithfulness of God in their lives. Meet their pastors, Dr. LeAnn Forrest and her husband, Karl, pastors of the Love & Truth Bible Community Church as they introduce them to good examples of fidelity and commitment and point them to faith in Christ. Know that where you start in life does not hinder the power of God to create for you a new future and to give you an expected end.

In a corner lot, tucked away, in a working class urbanized suburban community, "Flava Nuff, Flitters & Fry Fish," serves up all kinds of Jamaican delights. A community staple, this husband-and-wife couple, offers a safe haven to many families that need a warm meal, and a listening ear. A unique spot that boasts a community garden, a friendly breakfast, lunch, juice and desert counter, and a mini mart with grocery staples, it fulfills a stark need in this working class, diverse immigrant community.

Anthony and Stephanie Wright own the little patch of ground on which many miracles occur, miracles of broken hearts made whole, and families restored. Stephanie can often be found creating adventures for the community's children to mark every special holiday occasion. Families pay when they can what they can. Immigrants from Jamaica, Anthony from Bull Bay, Jamaica and Stephanie from inner city Kingston, in Alman town, they met when Anthony, after he finished culinary school in Brooklyn, which he put himself through, trucking over the summers, across the US, then became a cook for a major CruiseLine, that Stephanie had been on for her graduation celebration with her dear friend Melody.

With his promotion to head chef, he had the opportunity to travel all over the world, from Alaska, the rest of North America, South America, across to Europe, Asia, Africa and Australia. He loved being on the move, seeing what lay just beyond the next horizon.

Stephanie worked for the city transportation authority, while attending city college in Manhattan in the evenings, where she studied hospitality and Events Planning; then had the opportunity to work for the Federal Park's Department, overseeing special events, in Federal Parks across not only the continental US, but to travel to US territories all over the world.

Stephanie and Anthony enjoyed their friendship which bloomed as they shared the many exotic locations of their travels, but both careers focused, their paths did not cross each other in real time. They both loved nature, and beaches, and delighted in their adventurous lives, meeting new people, seeing new places.

Stephanie Mane had been in her late thirties, some ten years in her field, with a total of twenty years of government service, and starting to feel a little stir crazy. She wondered what her next would be, when she accepted an invitation to relax. Jamaicans from her inner-city Kingston community of Alman Town hosted their first reunion boat ride which her good friend, Melody, from over those many years since she first immigrated to this country, insisted that she come to Long Island to attend. The cool spring breeze danced across the marina as she boarded the party boat to the rhythmic pulsating sounds other favorite reggae artists blared through the airways.

Anthony, who had been invited to the same boat ride by his good friend, Fitzgerald who was also from Alman Town in Kingston, and who owned the trucking company that Anthony used to drive for to put himself through culinary school, felt excited to spend time with other Jamaicans. The sounds of home filled him with a familiarity as the reggae music drifted over the airways. Neither of them, not Stephanie nor Antony, had much family with which they were close, as their upbringing, when they were growing up as children in Jamaica had been so conflict ridden; Stephanie's parents had separated when she had still been a very young girl, and she ended up living with friends of her parents in Alman Town, who owned a grocery store, in inner city Kingston, and were also local politicians. Stephanie loved their big, long house, and all the activity, in the tightly packed community, with neighbors coming over, in and out.

Anthony grew up with his father's family, after his parents broke up, in Bull Bay, who owned a small farm that was a common tourist attraction, and also several mini busses. Pineapple trees lined the lot, mango trees, and a lot of other fruit trees evoked a sweet-smelling aroma on the property. Anthony remembers many warm days spent running over the small bridge to the tiny stream running through the farm. Anthony enjoyed growing up with his uncle, playing in the tree house, climbing the different trees to pick fruit and eat to his stomach's delight. He had been surrounded by so much nature, catching crayfish to make Peppa pot soup, and running around with the dogs and cats that could always be found on the property. It wasn't a big house, but it was a happy home.

Stephanie and Anthony had both taken the opportunity to come to this country on work exchange programs; Stephanie for an internship with the city government in their transportation arm, where she met her good friend also from her same community in Jamaica, Melody.

Anthony took the opportunity to become a driver for the trucking company of the owner, who would become his friend, Fitzgerald and not only his friend but his mentor, as he worked for him trucking, managing his warehouse where he had the trucks he owned, while going to school to study Culinary Arts. Stephanie had met her friend Melody, who lived on Long Island while they both worked in the city, her friend in the purchasing department for the city government office where Stephanie began her life in the States. On that early Spring boat ride, as they spent time together, Stephanie and Anthony, laughing and talking, very pleasantly surprised to see each other, they both instinctively knew they would take their friendship to another level, as they each felt the spark between them. Since Stephanie had been staying with her friend Melody, in West Babylon, while Anthony stayed with his friend, Fitzgerald in Brentwood, who now also owned a mechanic and car rental shop for exotic luxury cars, so they both chose to extend their stay to see where this new relationship would take them.

Anthony's friend did not let Anthony know that he had become very ill but finally told him of his condition when he knew he could hide it no longer, so Anthony knew he needed to go into early retirement to spend the time with his friend in his last remaining days, for his friend's life had grown a little hermit-like and solitary. Fitzgerald had been in a strained relationship with his own family that had gone on for too many years.

As single women, Stephanie and her friend, Melody enjoyed time together, Melody, also a mother, allowed Stephanie the opportunity to play aunt to both her sons, which she enjoyed, treasuring those moments. As Stephanie and Anthony started their new and exciting romantic relationship, Stephanie's friend, Melody invited her to church with her, as she had been a new believer herself, and worshiped at a family focused Bible based ministry, Love & Truth Bible Community Church.

Stephanie did not grow up going to church, but she was intrigued by this unusual ministry with its focus on family and faith. She invited her new romantic relationship to church with her and he didn't know what to expect either, as he too had not grown up going to church.

As they attended church, at Love & Truth, spent time together, they realized they had so much to learn, as they thought about their future together, a future they both wanted to have with each other and one which they desired would be stable, not broken like the childhood homes in which they grew up, with their parents both trying to get them from the other parent, bandied back and forth between them both, like a ping pong ball. They both reflected that though they missed growing up with their parents, they welcomed that they escaped the conflict. They knew they wouldn't want that turmoil and upheaval for their children, but how could they live a life of stability, when they had no model in their early, formative years? Their friendship with each other had them talk openly and honestly with one another. They shared their fears with each other, their dreams, their hope.

Anthony's friend, Fitzgerald died later that summer and left him his home and his businesses. Stephanie moved in with Anthony just after her birthday that October and they started going to relationship counsel with the pastor of their new church, Dr. LeAnne Forrest. Dr LeAnne became a mentor to Stephanie, she counseled her to let go of the past, to forgive her parents, and go boldly into her new future. A passionate couple, married for many decades, Stephanie and Anthony couldn't help but admire them, and welcomed the opportunity to learn as much as they could from them both. True dignitaries of solid character and integrity, the essence of royalty; Stephanie and Anthony were so very appreciative to have come to know them.

Visiting church with her friend, Melody, and living with her boyfriend, Anthony, Stephanie enjoyed life, which felt great, but something seemed to be missing; she still had no idea of her next. Stephanie wondered what the future held for her as she settled into her late thirties. She knew she wouldn't be going back to work for the government in Federal Parks as her life had come to a turning point and she wondered what lay around the next corner.

The Love & Truth Ladies Retreat proved to be a game changer as Stephanie found the answer to the question that she didn't realize she had been asking her whole life. Invited to the Women's Retreat with her new church, that late fall weekend evening, Stephanie gave her heart to the Lord and became a believer. She would never forget the message from Dr. Forrest, "Zion, God is calling you to a higher place of praise!" Her voice rang out as she preached a fiery message on the vessel marred in the Potter's Hand, and the Potter remade the vessel, He put it back on the wheel.

Stephanie thought about the disappointment that shrouded her heart with pain as she remembered her need to seek refuge in the home of family friends. She had often dismissed God as unresponsive to her heart's cry, all those years ago, in her early childhood. Could she really trust this Savior?

She determined to take the leap by faith and accept the Lord as her Savior. She believed in her heart and confessed with her mouth that God had raised Jesus from the dead.

Becoming a Christian began a new and exciting chapter in her life, there was so much though she had still yet to learn, but she had no idea that her whole life would change in the most wonderfully amazing way. Anthony asked Stephanie to marry him in a romantic Christmas proposal over a delicious breakfast he had cooked for the both of them with her favorite, ackee and saltfish, callaloo and fried dumpling. The Proposal marked the beginning of a brand-new chapter in her life.

A very small intimate Valentine's Day Wedding, lovely and romantic in Virginia Beach, took place in a rented cottage with a beautiful garden, attended by a few intimate and dear friends, with the people who had become so pivotal in their lives. Their pastors, The Forests, and their dear friend, Melody and both her sons, proved to be a lifeline, friends that they knew would forever become knitted as a crucial part of their lives moving into their new beginning, going forward. Melody invited them to this wonderful church, and for that they would forever be grateful.

The next three years gave birth to two pregnancies, twin boys, Caleb and Emmanuel, and 11 months later, the baby, Theo, along with Anthony had Stephanie immersed in her new life of being a wife and mother. There were some complications with the pregnancy with the twins, and the older of the twins, just by a few minutes, he had some challenges at birth. The younger twin seemed healthy and was so very protective of his twin brother and looked out for his younger brother as well. The three boys grew up together as triplets.

Stephanie encouraged Anthony to buy a new business, a deli spot, and mini-mart grocery, on a corner lot, when the boys started school, kindergarten and PreK, as they're only 11 months apart.

Now, celebrating 12 years of marriage, as Stephanie is about to be 50, and the children, the boys are getting ready to start Middle School, and their business together is entering its 7th year, they plan for the next phase of life, for expansion to buy property for a retreat space, right in their local community.

Their world is filled with wonder, and they have found contentment beyond all they could imagine or conceive. The Wright family has culled out their own little spot of harmony, which touches many lives with the power of kindness. As they look forward to continuing into the horizon together, their hearts remain knitted with each other, and with their God.

17

Marion and Albert's (June's) Love Story

In my senior year, my interest in boys spiraled and their interest in me seemed to spiral also. There were several boys at school that seemed to be trying to win my affection. Quite often, one of my suitors would visit. We'd sit on the sofa, watch television and talk, every now and then, one would hug me. That is, until my mom in the bedroom nearby would make this sound, as though she was clearing her throat. That was her way of letting me know it was time for my "date" to leave. She was very pleased though because before we moved to that part of the city, I was dating a boy that I told her I wanted to marry. We were just in middle school and loved each other very much but when my family moved, I lost interest in him. Most of my senior year I enjoyed the company of boys visiting until the two "Junes" came into my life.

The two Junes were best friends. Both were tall, at least six feet. (I am five feet four inches.) At school and in the neighborhood, they were called Black June and Bright June. That was because one was a dark mahogany skin tone and the other had a beige skin tone. They were always seen together.

Bright June would stop by my house, and we talked for a while. The next day, Black June stopped by. I had no idea then that they were actually betting on who would win my heart. Bright June surprised me one evening; he quickly stole a kiss. That was unexpected and rude. The next night Black June did the same. They were two ridiculous guys!

In school, I was sort of popular because classmates voted for me as their president or vice president in all our classes. I was also involved in practically every extracurricular activity that our school had to offer. In church, I was also actively involved.

Most of my courses were accelerated; like economics and algebra but social studies weren't. Way in the back of the class, where a group of boys sat that seemed to care very little about their education, sat Black June. I think he liked our teacher, Mr. Grant but I do not think he liked Social Studies, because he made a lot of terrible grades which didn't seem to bother him at all. One day in class, Mr. Grant was returning our test papers to us, and he yelled out very loud, "An F!" That made the whole class laugh.

One Saturday evening, the teenagers in our neighborhood went to a dance. We were all excited, laughing and joking around. The girls were walking a short distance ahead of the boys; and suddenly we heard scrambling noises from behind. It was a fight! All six or seven of the boys from the neighborhood were fighting with several other boys. No one knew who these other boys were, except me. I recognized Fred, my old boyfriend from the other side of town. All the girls screamed when we saw one of the boys fall to the ground, he was bleeding real bad. Fred and the other boys ran, seeing the police approaching. Black June was rushed to the hospital.

The news of the fight had spread around the school real fast. Everyone was questioning us about who were the other boys? What happened to cause the fight? How did they look? No one knew anything, but me. I told my mother about it and she warned me not to say anything. Her words were, "Don't get involved."

Black June was hospitalized for what seemed like a long time. One day during class, my Social Studies teacher, Mr. Grant, told me that, as the class president, it was my responsibility to visit Black June and let him know what we were studying in class. So, quite often, I boarded the bus after school and visited him. He was always happy to see me. We enjoyed each other's company. I really did not mind seeing him, I felt like that was the least I could do.

My family was so relieved when June was released from the hospital. Immediately after being discharged, he came to visit. He told us that he had gotten a bullet in his chest area and that the doctors would not take it out because it was too close to his lungs. Thank God he survived. My family loved him. Mom invited him to dinner, to our church, and to family gatherings. I sort of liked him too and we started going steady.

18

Ambrozine and Cyril's Love Story

I decided to include my grandparent's story in this book, after hearing about another book by Cristina Henriquez called "The Great Divide." It included a love story and a worker on the Panama Canal. It stirred up thoughts of my wonderful grandfather, who helped to build that canal. So here's the part of the story, I am able to pass on to my children and grands. Here we go . . .

Here is the story of a fair young maiden. She was shy and unassuming, who at the age of sixteen was sent to Panama by her mother Rachel, to help take care of her older sister Viola who had taken sick. Viola had traveled earlier to Panama to live and start her life.

Ambrozine's mother, Rachel Wilson, was born and raised in Barbados, West Indies and together with her husband Clark, had sixteen (16) children. Rachel was a businesswoman. She was one who from a young woman, bought and sold goods in the marketplace. She instilled many long-lasting values in her children, values that would be passed down and continue through the next generations.

This was now a difficult decision for Rachel to make to have her young daughter Ambrozine to leave her, but her sister needed her, and Rachel could not leave her many children to go and see about her older daughter.

Enter the story, Cyril Nurse. Cyril McDonald Nurse was born in Barbados, West Indies. His mother, Charlotte Bynoe, was born and raised in Brazil, South America. She was married to an East Indian man. Not sure of his name. They traveled to Barbados, where Cyril was born. As a young man, he would develop a trade in his country, and of course good values were also instilled in him as a child. He was also taught the ways of God. He had become a painter by trade, and it was because of his expertise, that Cyril was one of the many builders who helped to build the Panama Canal.

Ambrozine remained in Panama longer than she expected, but she knew that she needed to return home to help her mother and father with the other children. Now fate would take its course. Eventually she would meet her Prince Charming there.

Cyril would also do some painting on the side. At the same time Ambrozine was in town, Cyril was doing a painting job (part time) for a neighbor.

When Ambrozine took notice of him, she was bold enough to ask him to paint her sister's apartment. Cyril accepted the job.

Cyril and Ambrozine became friends and eventually, after much conversation and a reasonable period of time, he would ask for her hand in marriage. They were wed in the year of 1911. Now after he completed his assignment in the Panama Canal, Cyril and Ambrozine decided to move to the United States and settled in New York.

From this beautiful union, they had eleven beautiful children, only of which seven lived. They were Ruth, Donald, Ethna (mother's pet), Sylvia, St. Clair, Eileen, and Eleanor. Over the years, the children would refer to them as Mother and Papa. It was a very close-knit family.

During the depression, Mother would take piece work and ironing jobs in Bayridge. Every Saturday, Papa would go fishing in Sheepshead Bay in order to catch fish for Sunday dinner, and fish is what was eaten every Sunday.

Sunday dinner at Papa's house was a happy time. Everyone would sit together around the table. Papa didn't allow the children to laugh and talk during dinner, but after dinner they would talk, laugh and have a good time. Many evenings they would have story telling time with the whole family.

After the depression, times were a little better for the family. Papa would begin to work at the Post Office. He would also lose the tip of one of his fingers in a machine accident while holding that position. It has always been said that behind every good man, there is a good woman—well that was Mother, and whatever Papa said, she would swear to it.

Cyril had the hand of God on his life and would be helpful to a church at 880 Atlantic Avenue. He would often prepare the church for service and would light the wood stove to provide heat in the winter. The landlord of the building was a Jewish lady. She saw something in Papa, it was his faithfulness, and she would give him $1.00 weekly to help out his family.

Ambrozine, like her mother was a strong businesswoman and an entrepreneur. Not only did she handle the family business, paying bills etc., but she invested in real estate. Mother brought houses, keeping in mind her own children, so that they would not have to struggle in life.

Cyril and Ambrozine would also rent a house every summer down at Rockaway Beach. Just feet from the water, the family would relax there, swim and enjoy each other. That was a blessing each summer, because Mother knew how to handle finances, the family would reap the benefits. Auntie Sylvia's life was speared from drowning one year at that beach. They would also enjoy walking on the boardwalk. Some of their children and grandchildren would also get to enjoy the benefits of that summer rental in years following. Those were beautiful memories, made by at least the preceding two generations.

Papa continued to feel the call of God on his life. He answered that call and became a minister. He would often say, "Woe is me if I preach not the Gospel." Cyril became Pastor of Beulah Gospel Tabernacle in 1950. His family would always be in church, every Sunday, all day, and Tuesdays for prayer. Whenever Papa would leave the house, he would say "I go," and Mother would respond "God go with you." Mother worked close with Papa. She also worked in church, as the president of the Willing Workers. Ministry made them even closer. Their first two grandchildren were born two weeks apart, in that same year, to Sylvia and Alan Sr. and Donald Sr. and Julia. Obviously, it was a good year.

Mother was always taking people into her home if they needed help getting on their feet. She would not be found gossiping with the neighbors. They were always coming to her about their problems and talk of their personal business. When she was asked why she never talked about her business, her reply was simply "the only business I have is my children." Papa could trust his wife to keep the family together. The children also have never heard their parents' quarrel.

Papa loved the Word of God and could always be found reading it. He depended on God for everything—literally. If he asked God for something he would open Word of God to get the answer, and he got it directly. He was an upright man of God, and people always watched his life and admired his ways.

From their example, their children would mold their own lives and families. The Beulah Gospel Tabernacle still stands today and the children of Cyril and Ambrozine continue to work in that church. Two of their daughters made it to at least 100 years, and one of them is still counting. Grandchildren have also been part of that work from time to time. Their first granddaughter Beverly would teach Sunday School there and would be part of the junior ushers and play in the church band. She would also in her teenage years, preach the gospel as did her grandfather. They also had their first grandson Pastor Alan Plummer to preach in that same pulpit.

Mother passed away in May 1954 and Papa passed away

in October 1959. Their marriage lasted 43 years, until Mother passed away. They passed on a wonderful heritage. They created a great legacy for the family.

Homes purchased by Mother are now known as the Ambrozine Estates.

The original family home in Brooklyn, in later years sold for 2 million dollars. Their legacy is strong, they live it and will continue to pass it on!!!

The Beulah Gospel Tabernacle still stands today and the children of Cyril and Ambrozine continue to work in that church. Two of their daughters made it to at least 100 years, and one of them (Sylvia) is still counting. Grandchildren have also been part of that work from time to time. Their first granddaughter Beverly would teach Sunday School there and would be part of the junior ushers and play in the church band. She would also in her teenage years, preach the gospel as did her grandfather. They also had their first grandson Pastor Alan Plummer to preach in that same pulpit.

19

Aunt Sylvia and Uncle Alan's Love Story

Authentically told by Sylvia Nurse-Plummer
@ 102 years in July 2024

My story begins so many decades ago, about 77 years to be exact, however, I will never forget meeting my husband. It was the year 1947, just six years after the bombing of Pearl Harbor and two years after World War II had ended.

I interviewed my Aunt Sylvia at 101 years young times two. Once before I began this project, at a time when she was fully engaged in the story as she was flowing with more details, however, I didn't write anything down, so I made notes from my memory. The second time, I was intentional, this time armed with a recorder and witnesses. Even though her story took some detours, I found out a few things I never knew before, and some things were surprising.

I truly understand the importance of passing down our stories to the next generation, just so they will know, hear, appreciate and retell, even if they don't take heed. I tried to involve others in this process, but I realized this task was my responsibility, which I will share with love and dignity.

The Holy Bible is full of stories, legacy, precepts and more importantly examples, but if no one told them, I believe the generations would experience a bit more of troubles and struggles, then falling and failing.

Here's their story:

It started as any ordinary day. It was comfortably warm outside and no real clouds in the sky. That's when I met in whom I call today, "The Love of My Life." We were visiting another church for choir rehearsal. It was one of the local community choir rehearsals. Alan, was his name, sat across in the choir loft. I thought it was just like any other day in 1947. Remember I'm a PK (preacher's kid), but I had no idea that this rehearsal was going to change my life forever.

The group was not too large, so it wasn't too hard to pick out certain individuals. Of course, I only knew a couple of the young people. However, there was a young man there that caught my attention, little did I know I caught his eye too.

After choir rehearsal, as the group mixed and mingled. I could tell he had his eyes on me and so he came over and introduced himself. We spoke briefly and he began following me around, so we started to chat with each other a little more easily. He seemed so very nice, and he had a certain charm about him. His smile was contagious. We talked and laughed a little and we went our separate ways. That was our first conversation.

The next choir rehearsal was our second meeting. It was then he took my phone number, and that led to a few more conversations. As time when on, he asked me to have lunch with him on a Saturday. When I agreed, I knew of course he would have to go through the process of meeting family. Then if we were going to keep company outside of a church rehearsal, now more importantly, Alan would have to meet my parents, and I was not too sure how that would go. All I knew was Alan was kind, and he made me laugh. My father was the Pastor of Beulah Gospel Tabernacle in Brooklyn, so I knew he would have to undergo tough scrutiny. Besides I had an older brother, Donald, who was very protective of his five sisters.

From the first time I introduced him to my family, and as I recall, they absolutely loved him. He was so charming, and I felt my heart could relax a little, especially since he seemed to pass my Mother and Father test. Of course he was himself, and he seemed a little nervous, but still, he portrayed his charismatic posture.

Life was good and it was a sweet experience for me. I knew I had feelings for him, and I suppose he had feelings for me too. Alan told me "From the first time he saw me, he loved me." From that time, he pursued me. This quiet, reserved 24-year-old girl, who was a preacher's kid (PK) was very taken by his charm. We went out on a couple of dates together, along with other young people from the church. We always had a wonderful time. As our time and talks became more serious, the sound of marriage was on the horizon. I knew I would soon have to meet his parents, Mr. Adolf and Ms. Winfred Plummer.

I always dreamed of meeting a wonderful young man and I believed my dreams were coming true. I knew Alan was kind and loving. He never put his hands on me in a disrespectful or degrading manner, and he never tried to be inappropriate with me.

One day when we were alone at dinner, I guess he got up the nerve to ask me to marry him, and "to spend my life with him." My heart fluttered with excitement, but I can't remember what my answer was on that day.

After we became engaged to be married, there was a lot of planning that needed to take place. Luckily, I had four sisters, one of them was already married and thank God one of them could sew. I was blessed to have my sister Ethna make my wedding dress and also the dresses for my entire wedding party. I am hopeful that a picture of my dress will be in this book. It was unbelievably beautiful.

We were married in 1948, and the rest is history.

From the day we said "I do" we were inseparable. Married life was different for me, but enjoyable. We went on picnics in the park, we went to the beach and of course many other church events. We lived in a beautiful brownstone in Brooklyn, New York. It was there that my husband became a police officer by occupation, and he also developed a love for firefighting (he was actually a fire buff) during our life together. Many days while participating with the family, he would still listen to the status of any given fire in the area. When he would hear that it was a 3 or 4 alarm fire, off he would go to that site. He served as a police officer on the corner of Atlantic and Pennsylvania Aves, in Brooklyn, NY directing traffic there coming from five directions. Alan looked so very distinguished in his uniform and his bright white gloves.

We had our first son, my bundle of joy, Alan Jr. in January 1950. He was the first of our four beautiful children, three sons and one daughter, and the first male grandchild of my parents.

I had been working as a secretary/receptionist, so I had to take a leave to take care of my new husband and baby. This was my joy and responsibility, and I had great role models in my own parents. This was the family I loved, we were close, and I thank God every day for how God joined Alan and I together allowing us to have a wonderful life together.

Alan also loved to cook, so that meant he always helped me in the kitchen. At some point, in our lives, he took over some of the major cooking duties. He was good at that too. He was known for making a mean gravy. When rice was on the menu, everyone wanted him to cover "every grain" of rice with his gravy. It delighted him to do just that, and he smiled as he met each request.

Alan and I kept our family close and taught them the ways of God. We were close to our extended family also. Our children enjoyed the fellowship of their cousins, aunts and uncles. We went on picnic outings to places like Bear Mountain, Coney Island, and Rockaway beach. Even though we enjoyed some holidays at home, we would always connect with the rest of the family, many times just for dinner. I took care of my husband, my home and my children, as I had seen my mother do for her family while growing up. She was a great example.

We moved from Brooklyn in 1958, and my husband purchased a home for us in Hollis Queens and we began attending church at Bethel Gospel Tabernacle, under the leadership of Bishop Roderick R. and Gertrude Ceasar Sr. This was our new church home, and we attended church as a family. We were part of the Media Ministry and choir. Our children were part of the Youth for Christ. We basically became parents to the Youth for Christ Choir and began traveling with them, to church events, camp Joharie and many other places. My husband served until he became ill.

Before Alan's illness, it would be later in our marriage that he had also begun to work as a New York City Bus Driver, which he did until he retired.

What a life I shared with the love of my life until he left this earth. He was a wonderful man, father, friend and provider and took great care of our family. It has allowed me to live a comfortable life well into my senior years.

He made living, loving, and life at bit easier, always with God's help, a three-strand cord which would never be broken. Alan and I shared many wonderful days and nights with our immediate family. Our sons and daughter, were a blessing from God, never giving us any trouble. My husband was the "Priest" of our home, and he managed his position with humility, strength and wisdom. His sons have followed his priestly positioning in their own families, and our daughter knew just what posture to look for in a husband. This was a blessing to me.

20

Brenda and Tony's Love Story

I met a security guard at the IRS, a place where I was working part-time. He was very handsome, and I might add, he was quite muscular. As I entered each evening to go to my office, we would exchange simple pleasantries. Very soon our conversation started to be more than good morning or have a good evening. Once he found out my name, he began to greet me that way. There were times he saw me coming and he would move towards the door to open for me. Of course, I would graciously smile and say thank you.

One day I was running a little late for work and ran into a little commotion in the hallway. Well of course Mr. Security moved right in and moved me clear around what was going on. I was thankful. Later that day as I was leaving, we mention what was going on earlier. Right in the middle of our conversation, he made a comment about my outfit and my smile. He told me that my dress was beautiful and that it matched my beautiful smile. Now I was taken back a little. I think I may have blushed and tried my best to hurry away. I'm really thinking, "what is happening here?"

The next day was more of the same, however I felt a little awkward, but I smiled and said my usual greeting, but he held my attention for an extra few minutes with some general conversation. By now I was a little more comfortable with his comments and our conversations got a little longer.

As our conversation grew longer and a little deeper, it became apparent to me that he was interested in me, and I seemed to take a greater interest in him. When we spoke now, we were on a first name basis, and again it became clear to us that we were making a more serious connection.

Now even on my hectic days, he took a moment to make me smile. There were times when I came into the building, he would stare at me until our eyes met, and he would complement me, maybe to get my reaction. Then he would smile. Because I was not so much an outgoing person, I did not let on that I was not only smiling on the outside but inside too. My feelings for him were starting to grow a little also.

Shortly thereafter, I started a different day job and went to Toronto for three months. We simply did not talk during that time, mainly because cell phones did not exist then, and I did not call him the whole time I was in Canada. Actually, we had not exchanged home phone numbers at the time.

When I returned to Atlanta in September, I went back to my part-time job at the IRS. Wow! Tony was still there. I was happy to see him and he looked happy to see me also. Before I left for the day, he asked me for my phone number and told me that he missed seeing me at the job.

He called me that evening and talking to him in the evening became very regular, and almost every night I could count on his call. I really enjoyed our long talks. Then one day to my surprise, when I walked into work, Tony walked up to me and kissed me on my cheek. I remarked, "what was that for?" He replied, "because you're beautiful and I missed you." I was not expecting that, and I moved away quickly hoping no one else saw what had occurred. I wasn't sure how I felt, but as I sat at my desk, I smiled. That evening when he called, he asked me to go out on a date. I said yes of course. We planned to go out to dinner. We decided that we would meet at an Italian Restaurant in town, which at this writing, sadly, is no longer there.

I tried to make sure I put on one of my cutest outfits. I guess I was trying to impress him a little since it appeared that I had his attention. He said I looked fabulous. He was his usual handsome self, and now out of uniform, and I told him so. Our date went well and caused us to talk on the phone every night.

A week before Valentine's Day, he asked for the address to my day job. We didn't see each other for Valentine's Day, however when I saw him the next day, he asked me did I receive anything at my job. I told him I didn't, and he said that he had sent me flowers. I really didn't believe him. So, he said he had to go and take care of something. Even though I did not believe him, he followed up and had them to resend the flowers. So, I guess I was wrong, he really did send them.

Our dating relationship was pretty slow paced, but it was nice. He became a special part of my life. One evening he told me that he wanted us to get married. I wasn't expecting this either and it didn't seem like he was actually asking me the question. Well, you guessed it. Finally, the next night Tony asked me to marry him. He said this was in his mind for a while. I was hoping he would ask. I just didn't think it was going to be that night. He seemed like the kind of man I wanted in my life, for the rest of my life.

I believed he was the man for me, so I said yes. We were married on May 20, 1983, and our story continued for 32 beautiful years, until the love of my life passed away.

21

Debra and Alfred's Love Story

Divine Appointment by Debra Vaughn

Sometime in life we believe that things happen by happen stances. But as I got older I realized that isn't so. You may know the story of how Ruth met Boaz. It was because she refused to leave Naomi. I too met my Boaz through my cousin who introduced me to a friend who was known for many years by his family through the church. His mother and father knew my aunt and uncle and they were very good friends for years.

We took many trips together with the church, along with attending church dinners and all. Even with all those gatherings, we never formally met, even though we saw each other at church.

While attending a church function and along with God's timing, I was introduced to my husband to be, by my cousin at that function. We were very young, just 12 years old.

At that time, I was going through the pain of losing my grandfather who had cancer. Al would call me and check on me almost every evening to see how my grandfather was doing.

After his passing, he would call to check on me. From this point I felt he was a good friend.

I was about 12 at the time and he was a few months older than I. We began attending the church where his family and my aunt attended with the intention to join.

We then moved to the suburbs and his family had just done the same. We ended up living maybe three (3) miles away from each other. We went to the same high school, but he graduated first, and he went into the military.

We worked at the same hospital for few years. This caused us to see each other a lot. We always had long conversations, and he would call me most evenings, once I came home. We did go out for dinner on many occasions. I found him to be a kind man and a gentleman. Al was quite taller than I, so when we went out, I certainly felt safe with him, and found myself falling deeply in love with him. After a couple of years, experiencing each other's company, I believed he was the man I wanted to spend the rest of my life, so we got married.

Life was good as we made our way through life together. It was not always peaches and cream, I wanted to leave him a couple of times, even packed my bags, but God held us together through His great grace. I don't think we would have been good without each other because of the deep love that we shared. God blessed us with a baby girl. She held the heart of her father, and I gently held his heart.

Later we moved to Georgia where we have resided together for 56 years. I never left him, and I am so glad that part did not happen. I realized now every battle we didn't have to fight verbally but we fought them together on our knees and God worked it all out.

We had some storms in our life, such as the loss of our only daughter. God kept His promise to be with us through every situation. There were some tough days, but God allowed us to raise our four beautiful grandchildren, with faith and purpose. We are still learning. The grandchildren kept us young, and God is keeping our love on fire.

22

Diane and Clemet's Love Story

Back in the day, it wasn't considered taboo for two people to meet in a nightclub. In fact, that's exactly how my wife, Diane, and I met, and here we are, celebrating 42 years of marriage. You might say it was love at first dance—and I say "at first dance" because that's precisely how our story began.

I wasn't exactly the best dancer, but as soon as I walked into the club and took a seat at the bar, a lovely young lady approached me. She asked if I wanted to dance. One look at her, and I was on my feet, ready to head to the dance floor. That first dance was magical. Afterward, I joined her and her girlfriend at their table, and from that moment on, we spent nearly the entire night dancing.

The DJ, a good friend of mine, must have noticed the connection between us. He played a song by The Whispers, "And the Beat Goes On," multiple times that night. Little did we know that song would become a cherished anthem for us—a melody that would forever remind us of the night our love story began.

After dancing the night away, I invited Diane, her girlfriend, and my DJ friend to join me for breakfast. Wanting to make a great impression, I chose an exclusive restaurant in downtown New Orleans. There, we enjoyed a wonderful steak-and-egg breakfast, filled with laughter and conversation.

As the morning light crept in, I knew I wanted to see Diane again. I asked for her phone number, but she told me she didn't have a phone. So, I gave her my number instead, hopeful but uncertain if she would call. To my delight, my phone rang early the next morning. It was her—Diane Wilson. That call marked the beginning of our romance.

Fast forward 42 years, and Diane is not only my wife but my partner for life. Together, we have built a beautiful family with three children, ten grandchildren, and two great-grandchildren. We still enjoy dancing, and "And the Beat Goes On" remains our special song. Beyond that, we find joy in working together in our church and participating in its many activities.

Diane is my everything—my soulmate, my dance partner, my collaborator in faith, and my greatest blessing. Our journey began on a nightclub dance floor, but it has led us to a life filled with love, family, and shared purpose. Truly, the beat goes on.

23

Gabrielle and Lex's— My First Love Story

A Mature Outlook—The View Almost 20/20

On January 12 I got accepted into Savannah state university by the grace of God. I say by the grace of God because I didn't have the funds to go to school, but God said otherwise! I got to school a week late on January 16. My mom helped me to get settled in and started to leave the next day. I thought I was ready until she really said "alright" then the anxiety set in, and I realized she was leaving me. I started crying and so did she we cried all the way down to the car, and with tears down my face this boy with booty shorts on rides his bike pass us. In the mist of tears, I poked my mom and said "mom look at that boy with booty shorts on" as it was cold, and we had coats on. I guess I said it too loud because he turned back and looked at us but instead of mean mugging me and smiled. I finished saying my goodbyes to my mom and went on about my day. Some days after that I saw him again leaving a basketball game. He was staring at me, so I did the same, but I gave him the eyes. When I say the eyes, I mean a little bit of a seductive look to where he felt drawn to speak to me. I don't know exactly why I did it but when I got home, I gave myself a strange look, because I knew I wasn't attracted to him.

One day I told my roommate about the boy and how I'd never talk to someone like that. A couple days later my roommate and I went to a dance class and on the way there we saw him walking behind us. I told her "That's the guy that's him!!" She said, "yes that's Lex." We all took the elevator down and he said a couple of words to my roommate but nothing to me. When we got in the car to go to the dance class my roommate gets a call from her boyfriend. She then says that Lex wants to know my name, who I am, and what my Instagram is. I blushed and then my roommate told her boyfriend he'll have to ask me for all of that. So, we went to our dance class and had the time of our lives. When we got back to our dorm building Lex was outside walking back in the dorm. My roommate saw him and told me to hurry up and put lip gloss on before we got in the building. She was very adamant on it and it made me laugh. I put lip gloss on, and we walked in and there he was waiting by the elevator.

We all got in the elevator, and he spoke to my roommate a little. Then he spoke to me, and I was nervous because he looked like a mean boy. We walked to our rooms, and he told me his name was Lexington, and I told him my name was Gabrielle. We also exchanged Instagram's and spoke to each other that same night. From then we were connected of course there were ups and downs, but we stuck through it! Fast forward all the way up till today January 25, 2025, we are not together. He went to chase his dreams and football career, and I let him go. Even though I'm hurt I definitely think God will either improve him and bring us back together or bring me a better man. Only time will tell!

24

Addie and Norman's Love Story

This is our love story written on December 21, 2024, on our **60th anniversary.**

Our story begins:

It was one Sunday afternoon, late in the month of August, that Norman and I met for the first time. It was through Mary Joyce, who was one of my best friends. Now she had a boyfriend, and they decided to pay me a visit. Norman was with them. They said they had been out, just riding around and decided to stop by. That very day, Norman and I connected with each other and the next weekend, Norman came to visit me by himself. Right now, I don't believe he asked if he could stop by, but when Saturday came and to my surprise, there he was at my door, alone.

Norman was living in Ohio at the time, but he was in town visiting with his grandmother and family. He was 20 years old, but he would be 21 in September. My other observation was that he was fine as wine. I was 16, but I would turn 17 that November. After this visit with me, my dad was not happy about it, and he made it known to Norman that he did not have a daughter who was courting at this time. My dad clearly told Norman not to come back around again, and he left.

However, I guess my dad did not scare Norman off, because he was a little persistent and returned to my home the very next week. Maybe my dad forgot what he had told Norman, about not having a courting daughter, because nothing else was said about it again. So there my love journey began, and the rest is history.

Norman started coming by quiet frequently and we found ourselves falling in love with each other. We never wanted to be apart from each other. Norman decided that he didn't want to leave me, so he made the decision not to go back to Ohio. So, he moved in with his grandparents in Woodland. Our relationship grew deeper, and he would come up to visit Friday, Saturday and Sunday and include on occasion, one day out of the week, if he could borrow someone's car.

I can't say that we went on a lot of dates, but we spent much of our time together at home or just riding around in the neighborhood. Norman was such a gentleman with me, and I was truly in love. This was during the year 1963 into May 1964. I graduated in May of 1964. We were inseparable. It was then that we decided that we wanted to spend the rest of our lives together. Even though we said that I knew he would still have run that thought pass my parents.

We made a plan to get jobs so that we could save our money to get married. On that Sunday night, the last week of May, we would say our goodbye's, knowing we would not see each other for the next four months. This was a sad time for us as we held each other and cried so much. My heart was breaking at the thought of being without Norman. However, we promised to write and to call every day that we were apart.

Norman got on a bus and left for California, and I got on a bus going to New York from Atlanta. We stayed focused and we both got jobs and began to save our money as we planned. By the time October 1964 came around, we decided that being apart for those months, was long enough. So, Norman got on a bus leaving California and headed to New York to be with the love of his life. The trip took him three long days. My heart swelled with anticipation of his visit. I met him at the bus station in the city. We were so overjoyed to see one another. We knew our love was real.

I found a room for Norman. It was a very cute place that had a kitchenette and a bath. Norman found a job working as a cook. He met an older gentleman that really took to him. Now he had a ride to work. We had plans, but so did our heavenly Father.

On December 21, 1964, which was a cold but beautiful snowy day, Norman and I got married. My dream came true, and now my heart was filled with happiness. Our hearts were joined together as one. We began our life now as husband and wife. What a loving feeling. In November 1965, we had saved enough money to buy our own house. God had smiled on us, and we were so happy.

We began to travel to different places. His mom and dad lived in Pennsylvania, so we visited them quite often. Five years later we welcomed our first-born son to our family. Our first bundle of joy, Norman Jr. We moved to Florida in 1976, just the three of us. God was still making a way for our beautiful family. After three weeks of being there, we brought our home in sunny Florida. We found a church home and with that we found many friends.

Then in 1977 we had another beautiful event, our baby girl Jennifer was born. Now wouldn't you know it, we didn't stop there, one year later, our second beautiful baby girl, Erica was born. God blessed us with three beautiful babies, and they have grown up to be such a wonderful blessing to Norman and I.

God has led us through this journey and has truly smiled on us. We smile too, when we think of the goodness of our Heavenly Father, and the many blessings that He has bestowed on our family. Our love for each other has remained strong and still growing.

25

Marliss and Jay's Love Story

"... If you give me 10 days and
I'll give you the rest of my life ..."

Here's how we met . . .

After a failed marriage and subsequent long-term relationship with someone I thought I grow old with, I had decided and declared that I was ending my pursuit of having a love live. I just lost hope that I would ever find my person. So, I became a serial dater. I dated many and plenty. One day, I remember having a random conversation with my mother where I shared my newfound status and shortly into our conversation, she stopped me mid-sentence and said let's pray! As she began to pray, she started asking God to do things for me that I had given up on myself. After she finished praying down heaven, I asked her, why on earth would you pray for something I just told you I didn't want?! She said, ". . . son, I just don't want you to grow up and end up alone like me." Pondering her wise words, I must admit her words fell on partially deaf ears! I dated as many women as my time would allow! I referred to that era of my life as my "Data Collection" phase! My desire was to date enough different women to add up to the image and desires that lived in my head. Let's just say I did my best to live to prove my mother's prayers and words wrong.

As fate would have it, while traveling to Los Angeles my god-brother's wedding, it just so happens that an old work friend, that I had lost contact with for nearly 10 years, was staying in the same hotel that wedding reception was being held. My friend and I spent several years working together in Atlanta suburb and he was originally from Spartanburg, South Carolina. So, seeing him in LA was something completely unexpected.

After exiting different elevators at nearly the same time, he and his family walking ahead of me, I walked behind him noticing his mannerisms seemed familiar along with his distinctive laugh, and his peculiar walk. I told the person I was walking with that I thought I knew him. My friend said, no way that couldn't be him all the way in LA and not Atlanta! I called his name out. It was him! My brother from another mother. We were both surprised, and his wife and kids were looking at us like who is this guy my dad is hugging? We laughed cried and promised we would stay in touch. That experience is now what we refer to as God's divine timing!

You may be asking yourself, what was he doing in LA in the first place? Well, the wedding that I was a part of, just so happen to be the weekend and the week leading up to the Thanksgiving holiday. This is where my long-lost friend was spending the night in Los Angeles before waking to continue with he and his family for the Thanksgiving holiday.

After catching up and meeting his wonderful family, he said to me, when I make it back to town, we must get together and hang out. We exchanged information and realized that we lived less than 5 miles from one another.

One Sunday evening he invited me over to watch the game and during our conversation he shared that he was turning forty and wanted me to attend his birthday party he was having in Las Vegas! With no hesitation, I responded, "I'm there!" I was heavy on the dating scene at the time, not searching for anything long term but was open to likeminded companionship. As the time progressed and plans were set and agreed upon, I thought it would be a great idea to invite an ex-girlfriend (high school sweetheart) of mine on the trip to see if there was a chance to rekindle what we had as teenagers to see if it worked for us as responsible adults. Long story short, it didn't!

After four days celebrating my friend's fortieth birthday, my ex left and flew home and I wanted to spend my last day in Vegas doing what I love, taking it easy while people watching on the strip! A couple of the guys saw me in the lobby of our hotel and decided to join me. They were doing their very best to mix and mingle with the people near our outdoor table. Off in the distance across the street I saw these two black beautiful women walking towards our restaurant. I said to myself, if they walk in here, I am sending them another round of whatever they were enjoying.

Off in the distance, I heard our waitress bring beverages to the table and say, "This round is on Jay!" They both shouted in laughter, "Who's Jay?!" I tried to remain incognito but, the ladies insisted I join their table. I did so with a bit of reluctancy, I didn't want the guys that I was with to see what captured my interest and potentially ruin my chances. There I was sitting across from two beautiful cousins. One was from South Carolina and the other from Washington D.C. but living in LA. What was merely meant to be a gentlemanly gesture ended up lasting seven hours! Yes, you read that right seven hours, 3 servers, and an expensive bill I knew I had found my wife!

We talked about life, love, desires, religion, politics, you name it we covered it! It was like in an instant God had put my person across from me and it was three hours into our conversation that I knew I wanted it to last a lifetime. I remember it was about sunset and we both got up and decided that we needed to go to the restroom. On our way to the restroom. I felt like a proud man that was escorting the most beautiful woman to the restroom.

On our way back to the table, the sun was shining in the real bright, so she took my hand, and I led her back to the table. At that moment, I heard God say this is your wife. I said God there is absolutely no way anybody comes to Vegas and meets their wife. She's beautiful, but you know me and my thoughts on marriage. (What I now believe, God must've laughed at my naivety.) At the conclusion of the seven hours, we exchanged contact information, and I said to my future wife, "*. . . If you give me 10 days, I'll give you the rest of my life . . .*"

The next morning, she returned to LA, and I returned to Atlanta with a mission to prepare for my next chapter.

How I Fell in Love

I'm not one to believe in fairytales, prior to meeting my wife I would have told you, the concept of love at first sight is something that only existed movies. Somehow upon one encounter and initial interaction that I had found my person, and I was 100% sure that I was getting married again and to her. With the exception of approximately two-three weeks we didn't communicate. Clearing up my single life wasn't as easy as I anticipated but, outside of that, we talked every day! We laughed, joked and picked up like we were in Vegas. It was like I knew her my whole life. It was as if loving her came as easy as meeting her. We just clicked right from the gate!

A year later we returned to Vegas to commemorate our first meeting and left engaged to be married.

If there are no perfect people, there are no perfect marriages! You only withdraw what you deposit.

Although we had a fairytale meeting, planned a beautiful wedding, and welcomed a wonderful child our road travelled hadn't been easy. My wife's decision to leave LA cost her plenty of opportunities to work being in the field of entertainment. My first marriage ended cantankerously and with an almost teenage son, it became increasingly clear that I needed my son to see what real healthy love looked like modeled right in front of him. Within four years of meeting, my wife became a bonus mom, wife, and new mother all while trying to adjust to our new normal. Then grief hit our house in a real way with the sudden loss of my wife's father.

I am here to tell you grief does not have an alarm clock that will signal break time or end of shift. It is constant and if you've never loved while grieving, let me be the first to tell you it will not only change you, but, also, cause you to lose yourself all while trying to find who you are after losing a loving, impactful, and present parent!

I nearly lost my marriage believing that being present meant just being home! We were active in ministry but, hurting. We were the couple that people looked to for strength and direction but, we were lost and locked in our own stages of grief. The church where we served literally dropped us during our sabbatical, all in the midst of a global pandemic.

Feeling let down by God by not having our prayers answered in our own desires. I learned a valuable lesson in the ministry of presence. In this ministry you don't have to be brilliant, persuasive, articulate, or ordained or certified! You just have to be available for God to use you by the leading of God, Himself. As much as I felt ill equipped to navigate the trajectory my family was headed, I knew God blessed me with more than I deserved, and I was determined to save my marriage and family with Him navigating, directing and with His guiding wisdom.

At one of our darkest bouts of despair, that's where God's light shined on our marriage. It wasn't by words or deeds that saved us, but by love in action, empathy when it was needed.

The same patience God gives us, is the same grace we should give one another when we're experiencing emotions that we may not have ever faced. The ministry of presence taught me that you don't have to have a PhD in knowing what to say or do but, model God's love by showing up and just being there.

Message to My Younger Self

A message to my younger self would be, don't be afraid of being the first to do something. When God gives you vision to do something, He gave it to you! He trusted the idea with you! God trusts you enough to follow through on what He has creatively given you to do.

Also, don't be so hard on yourself, the world's criticisms are hard enough, don't join in and help, be the voice that calm's the doubt and call on the one who can calm all fears. God chose you and made you to be you!

Finally, life is like an EKG machine, as long as you have life in your body you will experience ups and downs! Just remember the one who brought you through the last time, is more than able to do something again!

A Message to Pass on to the Next Generation

Love is not a destination it's a journey! Fall in love with the process of doing, not the aspect of being. Simply put, love is an action verb. If someone says they love you, there should be some proof. I don't mean the purchase of a Berkin bag, or Chole clutch, or new latest pair of J's . . . I mean, are you present when your significant other needs you most? Don't let life become too busy that you abandon what you need to be successful interpersonally, collectively, and professionally.

I encourage you to create a relationship report card when times are good. Then when times get hard and you're not really sure of what you should be doing, you can revert back to your relationship report card to know what each person should be working on and contributing to the relationship. Have those relationship check ins that matter, not just for surface, or just to make sure that you're okay, but that you're both whole emotionally, physically and spiritually.

Expectations Manifest from Doing the Work

Celebrate every win, celebrate every accomplishment, and celebrate every anniversary. Each victory you celebrate is a sign of progress. This year we are blessed to celebrate eleven years together, ten years engaged, and nine years married. God has helped us and blessed us to make it this far. I'm also praying that he gives us the tools that we will need when we face challenges that we may not know how to overcome. I pray that He will equip us with the tools to continually say and model the example of I can, I will and conclude with *"I Do."*

If you're not strategizing for a plan to win and excel collectively and personally, you're modeling a plan to fail. If marriage on paper is a contract, then quite possibly your marriage is a business. Find out what you do well together and create a business so you can create legacy for your family for generations to come.

Scripture teaches us, *"For our light and momentary troubles are achieving for us an eternal glory that far outweighs them all. So, we fix our eyes not on what is seen, but on what is unseen, since what is seen is temporary, but what is unseen is eternal."*—*2 Corinthians*

You may ask, what is naturally eternal? The answer will be the legacy you leave.

My final thought, "you can teach someone how to love you based on how well you love you."

Celebrating Full Gospel Pastors

**Bishop Paul S. Morton & Pastor Debra B. Morton
Overseers Greater St. Stephens & Changing a Generation
Full Gospel Baptist Church**

As of 2024 married 48 years and going strong!

They have been doing ministry together for many years, bringing the Full Gospel Fellowship into being. They have been part of a multitude of community projects. Bishop Morton has won several Grammy Awards, and they have both written several books. Pastor Debra credits her husband for speaking over her life and being her covering and a wonderful partner in life. He keeps her grounded and makes her laugh. Together they raised four children that have followed them through the years in ministry, but now branching out in their own successful careers. They both love spoiling their grandchildren.

FULL GOSPEL BAPTIST CHURCH FELLOWSHIP INTERNATIONAL
BISHOP PAUL S. &
OVERSEER DEBRA
MORTON
HAPPY 46TH
ANNIVERSARY

Celebrating My Favorite Cousin

Pastor Alan Plummer Jr. and wife Sheila
Pastor—Counselor Entrepreneur

As of 2024 they have been married 51 years.

They were married in 1973. As young adults they attended the same church and participated with the youth and choir ministries. After they married, they continued in ministry together, counseling and married couples' ministries. Also became partners in business and in life. Raising four beautiful and successful children.

As of 2024 they have been married 51 years, and the beat goes on.

Celebrating My Best Friends and Superheroes

Abraham Ganz and wife Carmen
Married 60 years

This is a couple walked through this life with love, dedication to one another and service to their community and beyond. They were a true example of what marriage and family should look like. They raised their three beautiful daughters with great love and care. They exhibited that same loving care for their grandchildren. They were known throughout their close community of Copiague, New York. Their hospitality was infectious. Abraham was a hard worker and a symbol of strength to his large extended family. If they called you friend, you were a friend indeed. Their name was well known throughout Copiague, Puerta Rico and Australia. People took notice. This couple lived, laughed and loved together and on purpose. Everyone could tell they were loved, and they loved each other. At 90 years young, Carmen shares her many memories of their life with her beautiful grandchildren after losing the love of her life in 2024.

Celebrating My Former Pastors— Amityville Full Gospel Tabernacle

Bishop William Howard Walker Sr. and wife—Founders Married 65 years

As a young couple, they embraced ministry together. In 1960, Deacon Walker and his wife were sent by Bishop Roderick R. Caesar Sr. to the small town of Amityville, to pastor a new branch church. As they raised their four young beautiful children together, their names were known throughout their community, over the years holding many tent revivals and street services. After outgrowing their humble beginnings, they built a large edifice on that same property. Pastor William H. Walker had the support of his close family, as he endeavored to bring the gospel to a dying world. He was a devout man of prayer. He could be heard praying many long hours in the sanctuary, for the people of God. His prayer life showed immeasurable results as his legacy produced many renowned pastors and leaders, who would continue to spread the gospel of Jesus Christ. This included his youngest son, William. His lovely wife, Beatrice served by his side, and was a living example to young women. She was a "giver," especially to those in need. Still at the age of 92, she continued to serve as church mother, nurturing women, even after the passing of the love of her life. Mother Beatrice was a RN by profession and a gifted Bible instructor, who taught classes at the Bethel Bible Institute extension in Amityville, (AGFT). Through sickness and health, their love never failed each other.

Celebrating My Friends and Superheroes

Christian Church Members
Andre and wife Bonnie Isabelle
Married 62 years

This is a couple that gracefully walked through this life with love, faithfulness and dedication to one another. They were a true example of what a marriage relationship should look like. As they raised their four children together, their names were known throughout their community. They were the same in and out of their home. Andre covered his wife and his children in unmistakable grandeur and strength, and the world around them took notice. This is a couple that held hands wherever they walked together. He watched over his queen. As close as they were in this life, only a few days separated them in death. Family and friends funeralized them together, and they came out to support the family in record numbers. Everyone could tell they were loved, and they loved each other.

They were carried to their final resting place side by side and in grand style. Passed in 2025.